DAGDA'S DAUGHTER

RAVEN AND HUMMINGBIRD

BOOK TWO

NIKKI BROADWELL

AIRMID PUBLISHING
TUCSON, ARIZONA

Dagda's Daughter

Copyright © 2019
All rights reserved.

ISBN: 978-1-7326173-4-6

Formatting by: Polgarus Studio
Cover design by: Daniela Colleo—www.stunningbookcovers.com

OTHER BOOKS BY NIKKI:

Wolfmoon series:
Moonstone-Book 1
Willow-Book 2
Raven-Book 3
Faery-Book 4

Gypsy series: A Time Traveling Romance
Gypsy's Quest-Book 1
Gypsy's Return-Book 2
Gypsy's Secret-Book 3

Coyote series:
Just Another Desert Sunset
Coyote Sunrise

Summer McCloud paranormal murder series:
Murder in Plain Sight
Saffron and Seaweed
Black and White and *Red* all over
Finlay's Folly
The Night of the Jaguar
The Case of Missing Books

The Bridge
Time Gap

A Witch in Time Saves Nine
The moon in Her Eyes

The Last Keeper of the Light

Rosemary for Remembrance

Burning Night

Siobhan's Secret—book 1 of
Raven and Hummingbird series

Life is simply a dance that transforms us, loving, erotic and monstrous, it holds us in its web until the moment we return to begin again.

PROLOGUE

A present filled with a sense of loss, a life deadened by the Celtic god, Dagda's, whims. Ravens flit through her memory, reminding Katel of something…a past she cannot recall. Dagda is Katel's father, a being without scruples who has decided to take what he wants and damn the consequences. With his decision to leave Otherworld to live among humans, he has brought a spreading darkness that has now infiltrated the crossroads where the two realms intersect. What once was beautiful has become dangerous, forces never seen before finding their way up from the depths and into the light. With his treachery Dagda has loosed a future so bleak that not only Otherworld, but also earth will succumb. But what he doesn't know is that Katel is far more powerful than he ever could have dreamed. Her destiny is entwined with his, and her fate is to untangle the unnatural threads he has knotted together. But in order to do that she must remember…everything.

1

Oagda gazed out the picture window that overlooked the city, admiring the view. Brick and glass Arts and Craft style architecture dotted the cityscape, the buildings adding a special grace to the vista. It was nearly as beautiful as Otherworld, he thought to himself. The leaves of mature oaks and sycamore trees swayed in the breeze, cloud shadows racing across an otherwise pellucid sky. He smiled, his mind returning as it always did to his perfect situation. Being the CEO of a major corporation was what he'd been born to do. It had taken him all of five minutes to convince the ones in charge that he was the man for the job. Being a god living on earth definitely had its perks. Since that fateful day he'd bought the company, ousting those he didn't like and replacing them with men he'd hand-picked for the job; mercenaries out for money who would do his bidding.

A soft knock brought him out of his reverie. "Come!" he bellowed, moving behind his desk.

"Sorry to disturb you, sir," the mousy, bespectacled woman murmured, moving into the room. "But we have a situation that requires your attention." She moved forward to place a sheaf of papers on his desk. "First quarter earnings are looking good, but there is one slight hitch."

"And what is that?" he asked, glancing down at the papers.

"New competition, sir. We are no longer the only game in town."

"Well, in that case," he said, frowning, "get hold of the team and set up a meeting for this afternoon."

"Yes, sir," she said, backing out and closing the door behind her.

Dagda pressed his lips together and shook his head. Humans were so quick to fear the worst. Luckily the men and women he'd handpicked for his team were a bunch of cutthroats who only cared about the bottom line. In this world corporations were where the power was solidified—power that could be used politically. He chuckled, thinking about the congress that now ate out of his hand. If he ran for president, he would win hands down.

When the Celtic knot ring on his finger caught the light, he had a moment of misgiving, his thoughts going to his wife, Siobhan. She was heavy with his child, the second one he'd bestowed upon her. Siobhan had little memory of the first life the two of them had shared together, or the baby girl she'd given birth to. In her mind the baby she carried was her first. And he'd made her young again, in her best childbearing years.

Despite the woman being his creation, she retained her earlier sweetness and sense of right and wrong. Thank goodness this try had worked—his first try at resurrection had failed miserably, causing problems he was still dealing with. He imagined her in his mind's eye, her beautiful hazel eyes and sweet smile; his heart contracted with love, the feelings for her overwhelming in their intensity. If she ever discovered the treachery that ran rampant through his company, she would be furious with him. Luckily, she didn't know anything about what he really did, her innate trust giving him free rein to conduct his life as he saw fit.

From there his mind turned to Katel, his first child with Siobhan. He'd bound her goddess powers and taken away her memories of the man she loved. Bran was a god, but not one Dagda wanted as a son-in-law, or the father of his grandchildren. Bran was too soft, too loving. Katel needed a stronger man, one who could navigate this world that was turning darker and more evil with each passing day; power was the name of the game and whoever Kat ended up with needed to be an expert at playing it. Several suitable candidates came to mind; he could think of at least two men in his employ who were the right age and handsome and smart enough to fit the bill. *She will be better off,* he told himself, trying to rationalize what he'd done and was planning to do.

Although living in another city, he spied on her from time to time; he had to bind her powers more often now that she had turned twenty-two. She seemed happy enough, but why she had a preteen boy living with her was perplexing. How had that come about? He would have to investigate further and find out what was going on. He had noticed that she was more difficult to locate these days. And when he did find her, he had to use stronger magic to constrain her strength. He chuckled, thinking about what a mighty goddess she would make if he ever unbound her powers. But when that would be, he didn't know—perhaps never, if his life here continued the way he hoped. Soon he would be a father again with another half-god child—a boy. And this time he would be around to raise him.

He still felt constriction around his chest whenever he thought about Katel, some remaining guilt always rising up in him until he slammed it back where it belonged. He let out a humorless chuckle. *Is Kat my conscience? I was nicer back then,* he thought, trying to let go of the shame that always accompanied his forays into the past. Luckily the team chose that moment to arrive, their entrance into his office bringing his attention back to the present. He breathed out a heavy sigh and turned to deal with the problem at hand.

2

"What on earth have you done?" Kat stared at the mangy sheepdog eating from a bowl in her tiny kitchen.

Brant looked up from where he kneeled next to the black and white mutt that looked as though it had fleas. "Thought you needed an animal," he said with a grin. "Too quiet around here."

"For you, maybe," Kat replied, staring at her twelve-year-old charge. Why had she agreed to take this boy on? It had been less than a month and already he'd become her shadow. And when he wasn't dogging her every single place she went, he was doing things like this. According to Gwen, her boss who had arranged for Brant to live with her, the kid had no prospects, his drug addicted mother living on the street. He didn't act like any kid she'd ever known, with his extensive vocabulary and self-assurance. How could a child brought up in a homeless shelter and out in the woods by an uneducated drug addict know so much? She let out a heavy sigh. "I'm not home enough to have a dog, Brant. Is he even housebroken?"

"It's a female and yes, she is. What shall we name her?"

Kat frowned and turned to put her groceries away. "*If we keep her, she's your responsibility.*"

"That's fine by me. Does that mean I get to name her too?"

Kat shoved a head of lettuce, asparagus, and a hunk of cheese into the refrigerator. "Whatever," she said, distracted as she always was by the strange emotions that often plagued her when she was in the presence of this boy. Before she knew what was happening, he had thrown his arms around her and was pressed against her in a hug.

"Thank you, Kat," he murmured.

Kat extricated herself and tried not to notice how her body felt. *For god's sake, Kat—he's twelve years,* she told herself, wondering what in hell was wrong with her. He was mature for his age, and she could see how handsome he would be when he reached adulthood, but that didn't change his current age and her role as mother. When she glanced at him, he was watching her as though he could read her thoughts, his mouth turned slightly up at the corners. *It's the eyes,* she thought to herself. *That gorgeous mossy color and the way he looks at me sometimes, as though he's in love with me.* She shook herself mentally. "What shall we have for dinner tonight?"

Brant did a one shoulder shrug and ran his hands through his tangled mass of shoulder length hair.

"How about you take a shower before we eat, okay?" Kat suggested.

Brant let out a chortle. "Whatever you say, *Mom.*"

"I'm not..."

He waved a hand in the air. "I know, I know—you're not my mom."

"I would have been ten when you were born."

He let out a laugh. "Her name is Pooka."

"What?"

"The dog's name is Pooka—she just told me."

"Ha ha—very funny. But it's a good enough name." *Oh crap did I just agree to keep it?*

"Yes, I think you did."

Kat stared at him. "Are you a mind reader?"

A flush moved into his cheeks. "Sometimes I can…I don't know what you'd call it…I just know things."

"You're psychic."

He shrugged. "Maybe—Mom always said I knew what she was going to say before she said it."

Kat waved him away. "Go take your shower and get out of my hair."

Once Brant was out of the kitchen, she let out a sigh of relief. It was hard having him around all the time. She barely had a moment to herself now, what with him coming with her to Cerridwen's Cosmetic Cauldron where she worked, and tagging after her when she took a walk or went to collect herbs in the bigger forests outside the city. She couldn't remember the last time she'd been alone. At night when she crawled into bed was the only time she had to herself, and because she lived in a studio apartment, even that wasn't really private with him sleeping on the couch behind the screen she'd bought. *How did Gwen talk me into this?* she asked herself for the millionth time. She'd just begun to date Cedar—the worst timing ever. And yet here she was.

The dog gave a bark, startling her out of her reverie. She'd completely forgotten about Pooka. "A bath and a flea dip," she whispered, reaching down to rub behind the dog's ears. Brant's tenor voice wafted from the bathroom, the words of the song he sang strange and unintelligible. Were all twelve-year-old's as odd as he was?

Fifteen minutes later Brant arrived in the kitchen, his hair wet and a towel wrapped around his hips. Did he delight in making her uncomfortable?

"Something smells good," he said, leaving drips across the floor as he moved to the stove where she was preparing an impromptu curry.

"Go get dressed," she told him, making sure not to look into those luminous eyes.

"Yes, ma'am."

She turned just in time to see him removing the towel, wondering if he did these little shows to embarrass her. Modesty was not in his vocabulary. When his eyes met hers, she turned quickly away, her cheeks flaming.

3

"He's so strange," Kat whispered into Gwen's ear. Gwen was her boss, the owner of Cerridwen's Cosmetic Cauldron, the natural face product store where she'd worked for nearly a year now. It was Gwen who had arranged for Brant to come live with Kat, citing his mother's inability to care for him, and counting on Kat's soft heart.

In reality the white-haired crone was Cerridwen, the goddess of transformation and inspiration, something that Kat had sort of known at one time, but since her memories had been stripped, she no longer remembered—along with many other things. "What has he done?" Gwen asked innocently.

Kat glanced toward the back room where she'd left Brant, hoping he was busy doing the assignments in the notebooks Gwen had provided.

"He's like flirting…or trying to embarrass me, or something."

Gwen chuckled. "Typical twelve-year-old boy."

Kat glanced toward the arched opening as Brant emerged. "Can we go collect herbs now? I'm bored," he whined.

"Not yet," Kat replied, turning to Gwen who for some

reason was here today. Normally she managed the store on her own—and she liked it that way.

"Go," Gwen said waving a hand. "I have to do the taxes."

"I wondered why you were here."

Gwen smiled at the boy. "Make sure you keep her safe," she said, winking.

Brant grinned the grin that always lit up his already beautiful eyes. "I always do," he replied.

Kat frowned at the two of them. She knew it was a running joke between them, but the idea of *him* taking care of *her* was ludicrous. "We have a dog now to take over that job," she muttered, clapping her hands. A second later Pooka appeared from the back room, her gaze expectant. Her fur was smooth, all mats and fleas gone. With Brant's help, Kat had bathed her in flea rid shampoo. Her coat still looked a bit dull, but with the good diet she was on she would soon be her shiny self.

"I need lavender and chamomile," Gwen said, "and if you can find it, some hazel bark. Too early for rosehips."

It was late spring now, the roses just beginning to bloom. The often-absent sun was out today and Kat longed to be in the woods far from the city, but having a companion along who talked incessantly was not her favorite thing. "I'll get what I can." She pulled out her phone and called the number for Uber.

"I'm going over there," Brant told her once they arrived at the hardwood forest near the homeless camp on the edge of the city.

Kat gazed at where he pointed. "But that's the homeless camp."

"Yeah, I know. I like talking to them."

"I'll take Pooka with me, then."

Brant nodded. "She knows what to do."

"Really? How do you know that?"

"Because she's not really a dog, she's more like a protection spirit."

Kat laughed. "You are too much."

He shrugged and headed off, his hands deep in the pockets of his low-slung shorts.

"Okay, it's you and me," Kat whispered, taking a trail she knew. It led into what she liked to think of as the magical part of the forest, the place where she could swear she heard fairies and tiny creatures whispering. The sun always shone there, despite what the weather was up to everywhere else. She couldn't remember how she'd discovered this place. Someone had brought her here, and led her down these shadowy trails to locate special herbs, but for some reason the person was nameless and faceless, a blank in her memory.

Pooka loped ahead, floppy ears alert as she stopped to sniff this or that. She had to be part sheepdog with her long black and white fur and intelligent brown eyes.

Kat hurried down the trail that Pooka chose, not surprised when she came to a cleared area with chamomile growing. She bent to add it to the basket slung over her arm. It was so nice to be on her own for a change where she could think and process all that had happened this past month. But instead of processing she was overtaken by a vision.

She was with Brant, but he was older—closer to her own age. He was handsome and attentive, his arm around her waist as they walked together under the trees. She knew they were heading toward a pond where they would strip off their clothes and go skinny-dipping. And after that they would make love in the tall grass. Pooka's bark snapped her out of it.

She shivered, her heart pounding. The idea of making love with the kid she was raising was disgusting and immoral. It was barely ten seconds later that a man was standing in front of her, the same one who'd bothered her several times in the past. But she hadn't seen him in a while, and never here. He was wide-shouldered and barrel chested with coal black hair and piercing eyes the color of the sky just before the stars appeared. Pooka snapped at his legs, her mouth curled back in an angry snarl. When the man kicked at her, Kat shouted, "Leave her alone!"

He moved closer, his hands making intricate patterns as his eyes pinned her like a bug. From her past experiences she knew that if she didn't run right now, she'd be rooted to the spot until he was finished with her. She moved backward away from him, stumbling in her haste. And when Pooka distracted him, taking his gaze from hers, she turned and ran. Behind her Pooka's growls grew even more ferocious, the man shouting at her in a language Kat couldn't understand. She heard the thunk of his boot connecting with Pooka, the whimper that came afterward.

Tears were streaming down her face by the time she burst out of the forest and sprinted to where Brant stood talking with a dark-haired woman.

They both turned, worried looks on their faces. "What's

wrong?" Brant asked.

"A man," she gasped…the guy who's bothered me before—he's in the forest and I think he hurt Pooka."

"The dog will be fine," the woman said with an expression of certainty.

Kat stared at the stranger. "Where is she then?"

"Here she comes," Brant called, running toward the dog who loped toward them. "Good girl," he whispered, rubbing her ears.

"See?" the woman said, smiling.

Kat took a closer look at the stranger who had befriended her charge. She was probably in her thirties, brown hair filled with leaves and twigs and tangled around her angular face. She was barefoot, a bunch of small leather pouches attached to the leather belt she was wearing around her loose brown tunic. She had the look of a sprite who lived in the trees, a goddess of the forest. Was she a member of the homeless camp?

"My name's Airmid—I live here. I can help you find the herbs you're looking for. You were lucky today…I suggest you take a buddy next time."

"Do you know who that man is?"

Airmid's eyes narrowed. "He is a bad man who wishes to do you harm. If you manage to keep away from him, he'll lose interest."

"I don't get it—lose interest in what?"

Airmid and Brant exchanged a look. "In harming you of course. I've seen his kind before."

"He's like my dad was. He wants control over everything," Brant added.

"You never mentioned your dad. Where does he live?"

He lifted one shoulder. "I don't know and I don't want to know."

Kat glanced at Airmid. "How do you two know each other?"

"Didn't Brant tell you? He and his mom lived at our homeless camp for a while."

Brant smiled, watching her. "Yeah. Airmid and my mom are friends."

Kat had a sort of deja-vu feeling for a moment before she pulled out her cell phone and punched in the numbers for an Uber to take them home.

When the car arrived twenty minutes later Kat headed toward it, her back to the conversation going on between Airmid and Brant. *"I'm going crazy,"* she heard Brant say. *"If something doesn't happen soon, I'm telling her."*

"Don't do that. If he gets any inkling that you're around he'll do something even more drastic."

"How did he fucking find us today? I've put up every protection spell I know."

When Kat reached the car, she turned to look back at them. She was at least a hundred feet away and she could still hear them as if they were standing right next to her. And what in the world were they talking about? She climbed into the backseat and waited, watching Airmid give Brant a hug before he sprinted toward the car with Pooka right on his heels. "Sorry. She thinks of me like her son," he said. climbing into the backseat next to her.

"You both know that man, don't you?" she whispered as the driver did a U-turn and took off down the gravel road.

Brant blanched. "I…we…yes, if he's the one I think he

is. He used to raid our camp when Mom and I lived here. He's dangerous."

"And what are you, some sort of magician?" she scoffed. "Protection spell?"

He frowned. "You were too far away to hear me clearly. What I said was Pooka is protecting you."

Kat knew what she heard, wondering why he was lying. "What is it you threatened to tell me?"

"Tell you?" His eyes widened in innocence.

"Yes, tell me—I heard you say that if something doesn't happen soon…"

"Oh that," he chuckled. "I was talking about my mom. She promised to come see me, and she hasn't done it yet."

Kat stared at him. "Whatever, Brant. But I don't tolerate lying." The rest of the trip was made in silence.

4

"Goddamn it!" Dagda roared. "How did she come up with that fucking puca? That creature is a protective spirit and next time I see it I'll kill it."

"What?"

Dagda turned to see his secretary staring at him with wide eyes. "Sorry you had to hear that, Beatrice. I'm dealing with another issue right now. What do you need?"

"The team is waiting instructions, sir. Shall I send Jones in?"

"Yes, please do."

She backed away and left the door open as she exited. A second later a sandy-haired man came in, waiting his instructions. "I have an extra assignment for you, Jones. This is off the books so don't mention it to the other team members. I need you to spy on someone. You'll wonder why when you see her, but I have my reasons."

"What exactly do you want to know, sir?"

"Track her trips to the woods and find out who the kid is who's living with her. You have your contacts with the police force—don't hesitate to use them. And if you get a chance to kill her fucking black and white dog, please do it."

"Kill it?"

"You heard me. Report back in a week." Dagda waved his hand in the air to dismiss him, turning to the papers on his desk.

When Dagda arrived home that evening Siobhan was in the throes of labor, her beautiful features contorted in pain.

"What the fuck?" he yelled. "You're not supposed to feel pain."

Siobhan's eyes welled with tears. "Labor is usually painful, Dag. At least that's what I've heard." She let out a moan and bent at the waist as Dagda looked on in confusion.

"But I made you so…what in hell is going on?"

"Can we go to the hospital now? I'm pretty sure the baby is coming."

"No hospitals—I thought I made that clear! They'll find out…I mean, didn't you call the midwife I recommended?"

"I prefer the hospital."

"No, Siobhan. I forbid it."

"But what if something goes wrong?"

Dagda frowned in bewilderment. "Nothing will go wrong, Siobhan. I won't let it."

"But…" she let out a long drawn out howl as her water broke. A second later she crumpled to the floor.

Dagda paced, staring at her. Her eyes were closed, her skin as pale as ash. Her hands clutched at her belly pressing against the loose dress, a grimace of pain on her face. He'd expected the birth to go without a hitch, the baby to arrive without any pain or stress whatsoever. This was not supposed to happen. What if…he had a moment of panic as he thought of the resurrection, wondering if he'd screwed something up…if this baby would even make it.

A second later her eyes popped open. "Something's wrong, Dag. I can feel it," she muttered. This time she was silent as she doubled up. Tears squeezed out of her eyes as the contraction went on and on. When it was over, she fell back panting, her hair damp with sweat.

He bent to her, his fingers on her wrist registering how faint her heartbeat had become. Dagda was frantic. He couldn't call on anyone from Otherworld since they were all after him for his crimes. Maybe the Norse realm. He thought hard, finally deciding on Frigg, the goddess of fertility and childbirth, the one who was married to Odin. She was adept in the Norse magic of seidr, a sorcery that could override whatever was going on with Siobhan. All he could think about was his son, the one he'd hoped would be his legacy.

He picked her up and disappeared into the ether, leaving behind a thick dark fog that drifted along the floor. As he traveled, Siobhan writhed in his arms, her shrill cries scaring him more than he cared to admit. By the time he reached the Norse realm where Odin resided, she had fallen unconscious and was bleeding. He banged on the castle door, tears running down his ravaged cheeks.

When the door opened Frigg was standing there, her dark eyes lighting on the woman in his arms.

"Can you save her?" he cried out.

"Come inside," she urged, leading the way to a bedchamber.

Dagda placed Siobhan on the wide bed made of live oak limbs, green leaves crowding as they grew toward the light streaming through the ceiling of glass. "She...she's my creation. She wasn't supposed to feel pain. I..."

"Quiet," Frigg murmured, bending over the still figure. She placed a hand on Siobhan's chest and closed her eyes. "Wait outside, Dagda. This is not a sight you should see."

"The baby?"

"I will do my best."

"But...he's..."

"Go!" Frigg ordered, her eyes sparking with fire.

Dagda left the room and wandered the castle halls, his thoughts turbulent and filled with terror. He loved Siobhan. She carried his son, his heir. She had to make it. If he lost her...and what about his child? He'd counted on this, had made sure that he gave her a boy child this time around, not another girl. He'd dreamt of raising him, imagining how it would be. He let out a howl and rushed out the heavy doors into the gardens. It was there that he ran into Odin.

"What in all the deity's names are *you* doing here?" the ruler of the Aesir bellowed.

Dagda took in the heavy gray beard, the one good eye that stared at him in fury. "I had to see Frigg—I brought my wife, my woman...she..."

"We all know what you've done, Dagda. And we do not approve. What you have wrought has caused a major rift in the realms. We are all in danger of being obliterated by your one selfish act."

Dagda stared into the distance. "I had to, Odin. You know what it is to love a woman. She carries our child."

"And you have brought her here, why?"

"She's in labor and it is not going well. I had no idea that…"

"That being raised from the dead might make her unable to bear a child? Now she lies in there on her deathbed and you…you talk about yourself. I should report you, but I have made up my mind to stay out of Otherworld business. I have enough to deal with regarding Asgard."

Dagda bowed his head. "Thank you for that."

"Don't thank me. You will come to justice, maybe not today or tomorrow, but eventually you will be caught and punished. It is the way of the fates and of destiny."

Dagda wiped angrily at his face, trying to get himself under control. It was humiliating to fall apart in front of one of the most powerful gods of all time. "I hoped that Frigg could use the magic of seidr to help Siobhan."

"This woman has already been tainted, Dagda. There is a limit to what seidr magic can do. You should have taken her to Freya, who is a master of the craft. My wife will do everything in her power, but she is not as versed in divination and sorcery."

Dagda let out a moan and turned away. "I can't lose her," he muttered. When he felt Odin's hand on his shoulder he turned, surprised.

"I can see that what you feel for her is true. But you should not have meddled in life and death. Now you will face the consequences for your actions. Despite my anger and dismay, I hope she survives, but if she does not, you will know the pain of what you've done."

"My child…my son…"

"She carries a boy? Did you make this happen?"

Dagda nodded.

Odin shook his shaggy head. "You are a fool who should have been content with what you had."

Dagda stared at the ground, the god's words echoing inside him. He'd been arrogant to assume that his seed would grow inside her and come to fruition without a hint of trouble.

Odin let out a hiss of annoyance and left Dagda alone, his imposing figure disappearing into the shadows under the trees.

It was another hour before Frigg appeared in the doorway, strands of blonde hair pulled free from her braid and hanging untidily around her pale face. She gestured for Dagda to come inside.

"She will survive, as will your son. But there will be a payment exacted for your actions."

"What payment?" he asked, hurrying after her toward the bedroom.

"You will know it when it happens."

"You won't tell me?"

Frigg paused in the doorway to the bedroom, smoothing her long hair back into its intricate configuration. "I am not privy to that information, Dagda. I only see glimpses of darkness in your future."

But Dagda didn't hear her as he rushed to the bed, gazing down on his sleeping son nestled against Siobhan's breast. Siobhan's eyes were closed, her lashes dark against her ashen face, purple bruises under them. He tenderly touched the baby's dark head, the hair soft under his fingers. "Miorbhaileach," he whispered as tears dripped from his eyes. "A miracle."

K at was in the woods gathering herbs when she heard a twig snap and the sound of a hissed expletive. Pooka's ears lifted, her body stilling as she listened. A second later the dog took off, plunging into the underbrush.

"Jesus Christ!" came a shout, a gunshot exploding into the silence a moment later.

"Pooka!" Kat shouted, running toward where the dog had gone. She stopped when Pooka appeared next to her seeming calm and uninjured. "What the hell happened?" she whispered. Pooka trotted off, glancing over her shoulder to make sure Kat was following her. When Brant appeared on the trail, Kat let out a sigh of relief. Not that the kid could have done anything at all to protect her, but it was just nice to see another human being. "Did you see anyone?" she asked him, trying to stop her hands from trembling.

He frowned. "No. Should I have?"

"There was someone—a man in the brush. Pooka went after him. You must have heard the gunshot."

"I did. It's why I came to find you."

Kat frowned. "You don't seem that concerned. I could have been killed."

Brant did his one shoulder shrug. "Pooka will protect you."

Kat glanced down at the not at all scary black and white dog that had stuck to her like glue for the past few days. "From a man with a gun? Doubtful, Brant."

Brant reached down to pat the dog. "She's not just a dog, Kat. I already told you she's a puka, a protection spirit."

"Oh right—how could I forget?" But something inside her resonated with the assessment, her gaze going to the dog, whose golden eyes met hers.

"Did you see who it was?"

Kat lifted her eyes to Brant's. "No. Maybe it was just some guy out hunting and the dog startled him."

"Maybe." Brant stuck his hands deep not his pockets and strolled back toward the road.

Kat followed slowly, buried feelings rising to the surface of her mind. There was something... a tingle moving through her as she saw glimpses of another life, glimpses of a man she loved, and...but just when she thought she'd caught the tendril and was reeling it in, it all disappeared.

The next morning Brant told Kat he wasn't feeling well, begging off from going to work with her. "But take the dog," he urged.

"I'm not taking the dog. I have enough to do without

dealing with walking her three times."

"Fine. I'll do it," he mumbled.

"He's getting stranger and stranger," Kat told Gwen when the older woman came by the shop to check on her.

"How so, dear?"

"He looks at me funny, and I know he's kidding, but he says that Pooka is a protection spirit. He's just odd."

"He was brought up on the street, Kat. You can't expect him to behave as other boys his age."

"And speaking of that, why doesn't he have any friends?"

Gwen sighed. "Introvert?"

Kat turned as a customer came in, hoping to continue their conversation later. Even Gwen seemed untrustworthy now, as though she was keeping some deep dark secret.

6

"There was definitely someone tracking Kat in the woods."

Airmid glanced at Bran soaking in her healing pool. She moved closer to sit on a rock. "Dagda?"

Bran shook his head. "Pooka went after the guy and scared him off, but I'm kind of worried. The guy had a gun."

"Do you think this is Dagda's doing?"

"Could be. It's been two months since he's done his number on Kat's memories. He could very well have hired someone to track her down to make it easier for him."

"Has she shown any signs of...?"

Bran frowned and shook his head. "No goddess powers have shown up yet. I'm sick of this persona Gwen chose for me, and I'm about to go crazy watching her undress and snooping when she's in the bath."

Airmid laughed, stretching her bare toes into the thick grass growing around her healing spring. "You're certainly taking chances, Bran. Maybe you should avoid such things."

"Are you kidding? It's the only thing I live for right now."

Airmid smiled and shook her head. "The more you keep her safe from Dagda's magic the faster she'll come back to herself."

"I know that. I just wish it would happen sooner rather than later. And for all I know, once she becomes the goddess she's meant to be, she might not be in love with me anymore. There's been a lot of water under the bridge."

"You can't think that way. She loved you once—why would it change?"

"She has this boyfriend now. I don't know if they're having sex or what, but when she doesn't get home until one in the morning I tend to freak out."

Airmid bent to pick some flowers, winding them into her thick hair. "Even if they are, it doesn't mean she won't love you once her memories return. She's in a different reality right now."

"I have to speak with Gwen. I don't want to do this anymore. It's too fucking painful."

"But if you aren't protecting her…"

"She has Pooka and I can watch over her as a raven. If that bastard comes around, I'll peck his fucking eyes out."

"Which bastard are we talking about?"

Bran scoffed. "Dagda. I wouldn't do anything to a human being who's dating her—what do you take me for?"

"You're pretty distraught, Bran. I've never seen you like this."

"Yeah—this is about as shitty as I've ever felt. I want Dagda to go down. Maybe as a raven I can track him. Can't believe he's still at large."

"At large." Airmid laughed. "Such an earth term. Remember what I said about hiding in plain sight? Think about what he would be good at."

"Politician, running a company…dictator?"

"Yes, exactly. Maybe check out the internet for news of new companies or politicians who have recently been elected."

Bran nodded. "Not a bad idea. I can use Kat's computer while she's out with that guy."

Bran climbed out of the pool and found his clothes. "I may be upset, but I'm still a god. I better go if I want to be there when she gets home."

"Good luck, and let me know what happens."

"Are you still hanging out with the homeless crowd near the woods?"

"Yes, when I'm not here trying to solve the problems that are now plaguing our realm. If you haven't noticed, Otherworld is weakening. Just another reason we have to find the Dagda."

Bran grimaced and then turned in a circle, a wind coming up and covering him in black feathers. An instant later he lifted into the sky on wide wings.

7

"Brant, are you here?" When Kat walked into the living room there was a rush of movement just before she saw him. "What are you doing? And why are there feathers all over the floor?"

"I...there was a raven stuck in the room. I had to chase him out."

Kat stared into space, the word raven sparking an odd feeling in her. "A raven..." She bent to pick up a feather, gazing at it in wonder. "I love ravens."

"I do too," Brant agreed, gathering a few feathers together to toss out the window.

Kat came out of her trance, trying to focus. "What did you do all day?"

He shrugged. "Read, took Pooka for two long walks. That's about it."

"What did you read?"

Brant seemed confused for a moment. "Hmm...a book?"

Kat laughed. "What book, Brant? Was it one of the workbooks?"

"Yeah—a workbook. How was the shop today?"

She thought about her conversation with Gwen, the older woman's insistence that Brant was normal considering what he'd been through. "Fine. Made a lot of sales," she finished, heading for the refrigerator. She noticed him watching her, something about the look on his face disturbing. For just an instant she saw a man superimposed over the boy, his jaw covered with scruffy hair, mossy eyes swirling. But when she turned to look at him, he was a boy again.

"What's wrong?" he asked, strolling toward her.

"Nothing," she said, opening the refrigerator to stare unseeing at what was inside it.

"Didn't look like nothing. Your skin went kind of ashy."

"Did it?"

"Hey, you want some help with dinner?" he asked, moving close.

When his arm brushed against hers, she moved away, worried by the tingle she felt. "You've never offered before. Can you cook?"

"A little. Mom was an alcoholic, remember? She wasn't interested in food. I had to make my own dinners."

Had Gwen told her that? She didn't think so. "I'm sorry about that—must have been hard."

"Yeah, but it was ok. At least she loved me."

"Do you miss her?" Kat asked, reaching for a head of broccoli.

"I miss being loved," he muttered.

Kat turned at his tone, her gaze meeting his. He looked beyond sad, his eyes glazed over with pain. The expression on his face seemed way older than twelve. "I'm sorry," she said, reaching to hug him. His arms went around her, his head resting against hers as he bent his lanky frame. "I can never fill her place in your life," she murmured. The hug had gone on a little too long when she pulled away. "Didn't you say she was coming to see you sometime soon?"

He shook his head and picked up a knife to cut up the broccoli.

Kat's boyfriend, Cedar, was beyond annoyed by her reluctance to leave a twelve-year-old boy at home alone. When he called her after work his tone was remote. "I'm trying one more time, Kat," he said. "If you turn me down this time I'm giving up."

Kat laughed but she knew he had a perfect right to be annoyed. This was the third time he'd tried to see her this month. "When and where?"

Cedar let out a long sigh. She could almost see him raking his fingers through his hair, the downward slant of his mouth. "Dinner on Saturday night at the bistro on the corner and then some alone time at my apartment. Do you think your charge can manage to take care of himself for a few hours?"

Kat had a prickly feeling all over. So far they hadn't had sex, but she knew he wanted to. The alone time sounded suspiciously like a plea for just that. When she glanced to the side, Brant was staring at her with a frown. She moved away and whispered into her phone. "Sounds good to me."

"I'll pick you up at seven," Cedar said before clicking off.

"What sounds good?" Brant asked.

"I'm going out with Cedar on Saturday night," she answered, trying not to sound defensive. She had a right to a life, didn't she? Cedar was nice enough and certainly good-looking. She needed her own life away from Brant and this dog, who stuck to her like glue.

"When will you be home?"

"I don't know!" she yelled, turning toward the stove.

When she looked for him later to tell him dinner was ready, he was huddled into a ball on the couch, his head in his hands. "What is wrong with you?"

He looked up at her, his eyes glazed with tears. "Nothing."

"If you don't want to tell me, fine, but I'm not going to sit here every night with you. I need a life."

He hugged his knees and looked away.

Why did she feel so incredibly guilty?

By the time Saturday arrived Kat had nearly called Cedar to cancel. Brant was acting weirder than he ever had before, his soulful looks making her very uncomfortable. When she came out of the bathroom with a towel wrapped around her body he was standing right outside the bathroom door, his hands deep in his pockets. "What if I don't feel well?" he asked her.

She put a hand on his forehead. "You don't have a fever."

"But..."

"Stop it, Brant. I'm going out, and that is that."

"If I'm gone when you come back it's your fault," he muttered.

She grabbed his shoulder as he was leaving her bedroom. "What did you just say?"

He pulled away, muttering something she couldn't hear. "You'd better not do something stupid, Brant. I mean it. This game you're playing is not going to get you what you want."

He turned, his eyes narrowing into slits. "How do you know what I want?"

Kat glared at him. "I know you're trying to manipulate me into staying here."

"That guy is a loser and wants only one thing."

Kat's mouth dropped open. "When have you even talked with him?"

When he shrugged and left the room, she opened her closet to find something suitable to wear. But when she came out later, Brant stared at her in horror. "That blouse is way too low cut and those jeans are too tight. He'll get the wrong idea."

She was about to tell him to mind his own business when there was a knock on the door. She hurried to answer it, Brant trailing along behind her. When she opened the door Cedar smiled, his hand reaching for hers. That is until he saw Brant standing right behind her. "What the fuck, kid?"

When Kat turned to see what he was looking at she saw Brant giving Cedar the finger. "Stop that right now!" she yelled.

She picked up her bag off the chair by the door. "See you in the morning, Brant—and don't wait up," she called.

"What the hell is wrong with that kid?" Cedar asked as they headed toward his car.

"I don't know. I'm beginning to regret taking him on."

"I've been regretting it for a long time," Cedar muttered, opening the passenger side door to let her in.

"You look luscious tonight," Cedar told her later in his apartment. They had shared a bottle of wine and Kat was feeling tipsy, her inhibitions disappearing as the bottle emptied. When he reached for her, she melted into his arms. Maybe it was time to do the deed—they'd been dating off and on for over four months. He had unbuttoned her blouse and was kissing her neck when she heard a screech, both of them looking up to see an enormous raven staring at them from outside the closed window.

Cedar jumped up and shouted at it, waving his hands to scare it away. But when the bird didn't move, he opened a drawer and pulled out a gun. "Get the fuck out of here!" he screamed. A second later the gun went off, glass shattering and black feathers scattering across the floor.

Kat jumped off the couch and ran toward the window, her heart in her throat. "You didn't shoot it, did you?"

"I think I nicked it," Cedar answered, staring at the broken glass. "That piece of filthy trash better not come back."

Tears pricked Kat's eyes, her tipsy state disappearing as she took in the blood on the windowsill and the mass of feathers. She turned on him in a rage. "Why would you do that, Cedar? And you just destroyed your window."

"You think I should let a raven sit on my window sill?"

Kat buttoned her blouse and picked up her bag, a sick feeling moving through her. "What harm was it doing?"

"I don't like them—they're bad luck."

"Is my never wanting to see you again bad enough luck?" She left him standing there as she flung the door open, pulling out her phone to call an Uber as she rushed down the stairwell.

When she got home the front door to her apartment was open, black feathers strewn across the floor, as well as a trail of blood. "Brant?"

There was no answer. When Pooka appeared from where she'd been sleeping on Kat's bed, Kat bent to hug her. "Where is he?"

The dog's liquid eyes met hers, gold swirling as Pooka stared at her with an expression that could only be described as sad.

8

"The boy is gone?"

Kat gazed at the older woman, her eyes welling. "I didn't know what to do. I thought he'd come back Where would he go?"

"What happened to cause him to leave, Kat?"

"How do I know? He's a crazy kid."

Gwen gazed into the distance, a worried expression on her face.

"Shall I report it to the police? I have a connection there now." Kat thought of Detective Johansson and his taciturn ways. He'd helped her immensely with her mother's murder case.

Gwen shook her head. "As I said before, we don't want child protective services involved. He's a savvy kid. He'll do okay."

"On the street?"

Gwen shrugged. "He's lived on the street before. Maybe he'll come back."

"I don't think so. He…he was mad at me for going out with Cedar."

"Are you two serious?"

"Not after last night. He shot a raven."

"He what?"

"A raven was sitting on his windowsill and he shot it—right through the glass."

Gwen's eyes went wide. "Did he kill it?"

"No, but I think he hurt it."

Gwen began to pace, her gaze opaque.

"And even stranger than that, when I got home there were feathers all over the floor and I saw some blood."

Gwen's hand moved to her mouth. "Oh, my gods." Her worried eyes met Kat's. "Ravens are shape shifters, Kat. They are the links between this world and…" she stopped herself and looked around wildly. "I have to get home."

"Links…what are you talking about?"

But Gwen had already gathered up her purse and was rushing out the door.

Kat was running down the street after Gwen when a customer arrived, her pursuit cut short as she turned back to wait on her. It was only later when she was alone that the entire scenario expanded in her mind. A raven had been shot and some kind of dark bird had left feathers all over her apartment, as well as blood. Her mind seemed to open for a second, some knowing making its way into her brain. But a second later a door slammed shut, whatever intuition she might have had, stuck stubbornly behind it.

Gwen did not return that day, nor did she return the next one or the day after that. Kat went to work in a daze and returned home to Pooka, both she and the dog unable to get used to Brant being gone. As much as he'd irritated her, she liked him and felt a bond that she couldn't explain. The raven scenario played over and over in her mind, worry plaguing her when she thought of the poor bird. And where was Brant? Was he living in some rat-infested alley? Why hadn't he come back?

Her sleep was fitful, filled with dark imagery that she couldn't quite grasp. It felt like something she'd forgotten was trying hard to come to the surface. Gwen had encouraged her to meditate, and she began anew, sitting for hours with her spine straight and trying to breathe regularly. But when all she saw was darkness, trees that had been hit by lightning, dead birds and forests that had been destroyed by disease, she had to quit. Whatever was bubbling up from her subconscious scared her.

The end of the month came and went and still no Gwen. Usually the woman gave her a paycheck around this time. She had no cell number for Gwen, no address for where she and her daughter lived.

On Saturday she closed up the shop and took Pooka on a foraging trip, calling an Uber to take her to the forests where she found the most herbs; she hadn't been for a long time and she missed it. When the driver dropped her off, she noticed that the homeless camp was gone, used needles and trash all that remained. She hurried away from the energy she felt lingering about the place, and followed Pooka onto the familiar trail.

The day was pleasant, spring turning rapidly into summer as the days grew longer. Soon it would be summer solstice, a time that her mom had made a big deal about, taking Kat into the woods and talking about energies and long-gone myths regarding the longest day of the year. "From this point onward, the days will begin to shorten, and the Oak king who rules the sun will be replaced by the Holly king who will prevail until the winter solstice when the darkness is at its zenith. If we lived back then we would light a bonfire to purify the environment; the smoke and ash is said to drive away any bad spirits."

Kat loved these stories, her imagination taking flight as she visualized the community gathered around the fire and the singing and the long simple dresses and ribbons in their hair.

Despite her worry about Brant her mood lifted as she inhaled the tang from the sun-heated leaves and grasses, her gaze lighting on the soft mosses and ferns growing around the base of the trees. She always had a sense that there was magic here, maybe fairies or tiny creatures that she couldn't see, watching her as she slipped by. But the atmosphere changed the further on she went. First it was Pooka who suddenly stopped in front of her, her nose lifted in the wind. Her hackles rose, a low growl coming from deep in her throat.

"What is it, girl?" Kat asked, peering ahead. What she saw made the hair on the back of her neck stand up. Instead of the sylvan, sun-drenched spaces between the trees, there was a muddy darkness, as though all the color had been leached away. Pooka glanced back before cautiously moving forward, slinking like the sheepdog she was. Kat followed.

When they came to the spot where she usually found the best herbs, the trees, grasses, and even the path she was on, changed into shades of gray, like a photograph done in black and white. A cold wind blew her hair back and she heard a soft moaning, whether from the wind or a person, she wasn't sure. Energies, like spiders, ran up her arms, her fingers brushing at them; but there was nothing there. "What is this place?" she whispered. When Pooka growled again Kat noticed that the dog had changed, her body more wolf-like and larger than it had been. A voice reached her, a shape wafting in the air. "Go from this place," the wispy indistinct figure said.

"Why? What is it?"

But the figure was gone, Pooka's golden amber eyes on the spot where she'd been. "This is a dream," Kat muttered. "It has to be." But she didn't wake up as she turned and fled, Pooka right behind her.

By the time Kat reached the apartment she'd talked herself into thinking that the entire experience had been brought on by lack of food and her wild imagination. There was no way a real forest could look like that. And that ghost-like figure? Ridiculous. She fed Pooka and sat on the couch, trying to rid herself of the sensations that ran through her body, and the voice in her head telling her things she didn't want to hear: *You are more than you think you are—what you saw was the truth of what is happening—you need to remember.* Remember what?

That night she dreamed about a raven, his downy head pressed into her palm, his eye sad as he regarded her solemnly. When she stroked his feathers, he made a choking sound, snuggling against her. He was warm and solid, his heart beating in rhythm with hers. When she woke she had tears running down her face. *Cedar shooting at that raven must have affected me more than I realized,* she said to herself. But when she found two dark feathers in the bed her mind stilled, her pulse pounding in her ears.

It was after breakfast when she heard a knock at the door. Hoping it was Brant she rushed to open it, surprised to see a strange man standing there. *Here it comes,* she thought, bracing herself. *He's going to tell me they found Brant's body.* But instead the man smiled. "Hello, ma'am. Just wondered if you'd like your windows washed."

Windows washed? Kat glanced around at her filthy windows, the smudges where a raven had pecked against the glass. "Well, they certainly need it, but I…"

"I don't charge much—maybe just a cup of coffee and some breakfast?"

Kat regarded the man dressed in expensive slacks and a polo shirt. His blonde hair was styled, the aroma of after shave wafting from his clean-shaven chin. "Are you serious?"

He grinned. "It's my good deed day. My name is Jones. I work for a window-washing company, but on Sundays I work pro bono." He pulled out his driver's license and showed her, also handing over a business card with Worry-free Window Washing Inc. printed on it.

She glanced at the card and back at him. He didn't have the vibe of a serial killer, although how would she know? "Come in," she said, swinging the door wide.

Kat watched him work from her place on the couch, finally deciding to cook some breakfast. It was about thirty minutes later that he arrived in the kitchen. "This window is the worst of all," he said, gazing at it.

She nodded, unlatching it. "A raven pecked at it a while back and I haven't had the time to…"

"Do you have a son?" the man asked, interrupting her.

Kat frowned. "I had a…a young border. Why do you ask?"

"I noticed some workbooks in the other room, and when you mentioned being busy, I…"

"He's gone," Kat said bluntly, turning to the French press. "Want a cup of coffee?"

"Sure—thanks. What happened to him?"

Kat gazed at the floor as she pressed the plunger down, nearly upsetting the pot. "He took off. He was a foster. His mother lives on the street."

"Hmm…" Jones rinsed his rag in the pail of soapy water and ran it across the inside of the glass. "How did you end up saddled with him?"

Kat chuckled. "My boss, Gwen, arranged it. I miss him, but oh my gosh—he was the strangest kid I've ever met."

Jones squeegeed the window and then soaped up the other side. "How so?"

"He seemed way older than his years and…" She stopped herself just in time from blurting out all the odd feelings she'd had about Brant. When she glanced at Jones, he was watching her, the squeegee held aloft. She shrugged and turned back to the stove.

As soon as the bacon was sizzling Pooka appeared from under her bed, her tongue lolling. "You beggar," she whispered. When she heard an intake of breath she glanced at Jones. "What's wrong?" she asked, noticing the strange expression on his face as he stared at the dog.

"Nothing," he muttered, turning back to the window.

The windows were completed by the time breakfast was cooked, both of them sitting down at her kitchen table to eat. "So how did you get into the window washing business?" she asked, forking eggs into her mouth.

He gazed into the distance for a moment before he said, "My father's company."

Kat was clearing the table when she noticed the holster underneath his shirt, the gun obvious just beneath his armpit. She froze in mid-stride, red flags going off in her brain. "Why are you carrying a gun?"

He stilled, his gazed fixed. A moment went by and then another before he finally said, "Force of habit. I used to be a cop."

Kat knew intuitively that this was a lie. When Pooka let out a growl she reached for her. "I suggest you get out of here before my dog attacks you."

He turned, his eyes wide with innocence. "Why would she do that?"

"Because you just lied to me and she knows you aren't who you say you are."

He stood, letting out a chuckle. "You have a great imagination, Katel. But if you feel that way I'll go. Thanks for breakfast."

Instead of thanking him for his work Kat hurried to the door and opened it, all her nerve endings telling her to get this man out of her apartment immediately. As soon as he was in the hall she closed and locked it, throwing the deadbolt across. Pooka stood beside her with hackles raised and eyes the same golden amber they'd been in the forest. Kat frowned, her thoughts on Jones. She hadn't told him her name—how did he know it?

Dagda leaned back in his chair. "She told you that a woman named Gwen arranged it?"

"That's what she said."

"Did she mention ravens?"

Jones nodded, running a hand across his chin. "A raven dirtied the window in the kitchen."

Dagda nodded, his eyes narrowing. "And the dog?"

"Normal sheepdog, although according to Katel, the dog didn't like me."

"And you didn't kill it as I ordered?"

Jones backed up a step. "Didn't think it was appropriate to pull out a gun in her apartment and shoot her dog."

"Don't you have any imagination?" Dagda shook his head, his lips forming a thin line. "Do it, Jones, and report back once it's done."

"But sir, who is this Katel? She seems just a normal young woman who…"

"That is none of your fucking business!" Dagda roared. "I didn't hire you to question me. If you expect to receive your extremely generous salary, I suggest you do what I ask." He waved his hand in dismissal, his gaze going to the stack of papers on his desk as Jones backed out and closed the door behind him.

Once Jones was gone Dagda's annoyance grew more intense, anger mottling his cheeks with red splotches. Jones was an idiot, unable to carry out the simplest orders. It seemed, from the mention of Gwen, that this boy was more than a stray. Gwen was a goddess, and he was sure she was working in tandem with Bran to bring Kat's memories back. He had to admit it was an ingenious plan—but where was Bran now? Several months had passed in which Dagda had been thwarted from making sure Kat was still under his control. "Goddamn it," he muttered, anger infusing him with a raw energy that made him pace his office like a caged lion.

His wife and newborn son were still in the Norse realm with Frigg, his control of that situation lost, and his mind adrift on a sea of misgivings. His ability to save her from pain had not come through as it should have, and she was still in danger. Frigg's abilities in seidr, the ancient sorcery, was not what he'd hoped. It had been nearly impossible for him to leave her there, Frigg's promise to call on Freya the one thing that gave him hope as he bent to kiss Siobhan's pale cheek and pressed a hand to his son's downy head. The baby took sustenance as Siobhan lay unconscious, unaware of the baby's existence or even the feel of him as he suckled.

He let out a low moan and stilled in front of the window. The weather had been terrible for days, clouds thick and a sickly gray yellow. It matched his mood perfectly. The worry of losing Siobhan was a constriction around his chest, slowly squeezing the life out of him. He couldn't concentrate on his business until he knew she was safe at home with their baby by her side.

Two days later he was on his way to Odin's castle, his heart in his throat. This time he'd taken his raven shape, soaring on the wind as he covered the vast distances that lay between earth and the Norse realm. Somehow his raven mind made better sense of what was happening above and below; the devastation that crept across both the mystical lands and earth was more obvious to his far-seeing bird eyes. It was his defection that was causing this, but he was unable to stop himself from continuing his life on earth. If he were to return to Otherworld his punishment would be severe. And as far as his wife and son, they would not be allowed to come with him. No, they would be left alone on earth to fend for themselves, without his support and love. He let out a caw of fury and pain, diving in a gust of wind in order to forget.

By the time Dagda reached the castle he was riven with guilt, a terrible fear taking him over. He'd never felt like this, had never experienced such love for another— especially a human. His heart beat erratically as he returned to his human shape, terrified of what he would find behind those heavy oak doors.

Freya's blonde hair shone like gold in the light sifting down from the translucent ceiling, her beautiful face contorted with worry. "She's still in danger, but at least she's awake now."

Dagda paused in the hall, afraid to ask the next question on his mind. "The baby...?"

Freya's expression lifted. "Baby is doing fine."

Dagda let out a heavy sigh, his shoulders dropping. "Frigg?"

"She's with Siobhan."

Dagda nodded, his eyes going dark with love. "Can I see them?"

Freya shook her head. "Not right now, Dagda." She pointed to a bench. "Wait here and she'll come and get you when it's time."

Dagda watched her leave, her silky dress swishing as she moved into the shadows. He sat heavily, his gaze going to the lit candles, the fire blazing in the fireplace. A long table had been set with silver and china, a bouquet of flowers in the middle. He realized suddenly that summer solstice was nearing, a time when Otherworld held their celebrations. He had always presided at the head of the table as the festivities wore into the long summer night. A pang of longing entered his heart, the beauty and soft light of Otherworld piercing him like a long-lost love. He missed the fireflies, the call of the night birds, the owls, and the laughter of the gods and goddesses as they came together for the bonfire. *If only*, he thought, the wish left hanging as he realized that the two worlds could never meet.

It wasn't long before he saw Frigg approaching, her lovely features pale and drawn. "Siobhan is asking for you."

He stood. "How is she?"

"She is diminished. It will be a long time before she can be a wife to you."

"I don't care about that. I want her to be healthy."

"I am glad to hear you say that. It has been plaguing her."

Dagda frowned. "She's worrying about my feelings, when she…?"

Frigg nodded. "She's seems to think it's a big part of your relationship, one that you have come to expect."

Dagda shook his head, bewilderment rising up. "Does she not enjoy it?"

Frigg smiled. "She does enjoy it. But because of what I've told her regarding her healing time, she expressed concern."

Dagda colored. "How long will it be?"

"It could take six months for her insides to be restored. She was resurrected and has had to be resurrected once again."

Dagda's eyes widened in alarm. "She died?"

Frigg nodded. "If it wasn't for Freya, she would not have made it. And because of this she is more fragile than before."

"What about taking care of a baby?"

"The baby does nothing but sleep and eat right now. As long as you feed her well, she will have the milk for him. But she must remain in bed. I suggest you bring her back here at Lughnasadh."

Lughnasadh, the harvest festival that honored Lugh, the sun god, a friend who Dagda was sure had turned his back on him, along with all the others. His expression had darkened when he felt Frigg's hand on his arm.

"She is anxious to see you."

He snapped out of it and followed her down the long hall and into the light filled bedroom.

Siobhan was like a fragile bird, the bones of her face prominent. Her silky red gold hair lay across the pale pillow like blood, her eyes sunken and dark. She held out her hand and he hurried to her, tears already dripping down his cheeks. He buried his face in her neck and sobbed.

"Look at your son," she whispered. "He takes after you."

Dagda raised his head to peer at the dark-haired being lying close by her.

The baby had grown since he'd last seen him, his skin ruddy and dark eyes flashing with knowing. "Miorbhaleach," he murmured bending to kiss the top of his head.

"What is that word, Dag?"

He smiled. "It means miracle. We will call him Mior."

Siobhan nodded, gazing on the baby. "He is a miracle, as am I."

Dagda studied her before turning to Frigg, his gaze questioning. "She knows, Dagda. She knows all of it now."

"I remember dying," Siobhan said, her voice weak with disuse. "But I don't remember the time in between. My awareness of all that was gone until I came here and died again." She smiled at Frigg. "If it hadn't been for these...goddesses, I..."

"You know they're goddesses?"

Siobhan let out a shaky laugh followed by a coughing fit. When it was under control her hazel gaze met his. "Could anyone lay eyes on Frigg and Freya and not know what they are?"

Dagda chuckled, some of his worry dissipating. It was a strain to keep it all a secret. "And it didn't frighten you?"

"I remember our first life together, the wonderful year we spent and the birth of our daughter. I was aware of what you were, but I chose not to tell you because I also knew you wouldn't be able to stay with us. If I'd told you, you would have agonized over what you had to do."

Dagda let out a sigh of relief, but when she asked her next question, his insides twisted with guilt.

"Where is our daughter, Dag? Where is Katel?"

10

Bran twisted his hair into a knot on the back of his head and stuck a stick through it. It was lank and dirty, longer than it had been in a century. He glanced around the darkening forest, a feeling of impending doom settling into his empty belly. After seeing Kat and Cedar together he'd headed back to Otherworld, some essential part of his being collapsing. She was with another man now, her memories of what they had together never coming back. And witnessing it had been one of the hardest things he'd ever had to do. He cradled his arm where the bullet had nicked him, the wound still tender. Thank goodness the asshole was a bad shot. He wondered how Kat had reacted to the shooting; he hadn't stayed around long enough to see. *No point in worrying about it*, he told himself. *That part of my life is done.*

"Please, Bran—you have to reconsider this ridiculous plan!" Airmid implored when he stopped by her spring to say goodbye.

"Otherworld is disintegrating around us and you're worried about me? I can't stay here and watch everything

I love drift away. Maybe the Norse realm will be safe longer, since it's farther from the epicenter of Dagda's debacle."

"You are being utterly selfish. All the gods and goddesses are meeting on a weekly basis to come up with a plan to stop this. Six gods are after Dagda now, including Forseti. Why don't you join them?"

"I want nothing to do with that bastard."

"And what about Kat? I thought you said you were making progress."

He shook his head, his eyes dark with pain. "I've given up on her. Pooka will protect her."

"But…you love her."

He held up his hand to stop her and shook his head. "I've suffered living with her. You have no idea of the pain I've felt watching her go out with that dude and seeing her succumb to his manipulations."

"They haven't…"

"How do I know? I can't stand it, Airmid."

"A soak before you go?" she invited, pointing to the water that had taken on a decidedly murky tone.

He glanced at the spring, his nose wrinkling. "Even your spring is being affected. How long before it's a fetid cesspool? What happens when this entire place is just a wasteland and the dark spirits have overrun Otherworld? No. I'm leaving today."

Airmid had tears in her eyes as she reached to hug him. "I hate this," she whispered. "I want it to be the way it was before…"

"Before Dagda fucked everything up?" he scoffed, pulling away. "May our paths cross again," he said, giving her one last lingering look before he transformed, the raven's dark wings widening to lift him into the air.

The sky went from blue to dark gray, storm clouds building as the raven flew. He had a vague idea of where he was going, his bird mind hazy but also instinctual. He knew the lay of the land, the signs that showed what was happening, not only in Otherworld, where he'd spent so many centuries, but on earth as well. He felt it in his bones, the beginning of something malevolent coming to life.

A long time passed before he reached the outskirts of Asgard, the realm of the Norse gods and goddesses. His feathers disappeared as he shifted into his god shape of Bran the Blessed. He was the god of ravens and prophecy, the legends of what he'd accomplished written down in the books that littered the libraries in the human world. He'd forgotten himself, forgotten his power and his abilities, his love for Kat overcoming everything he was and had been. It was time to embrace his power, embrace the fire that had always consumed him. To be the god he was meant to be— he must have a purpose in this timeline, he only needed to find it. But even as he thought these thoughts his heart yearned for the woman, yearned for what they'd had before Dagda ruined everything. Anger rose up in him, the desire to kill the all-father god consuming him. He had to get beyond this, had to reclaim his strength and let go of what could never be.

He let out a heavy sigh, his gaze on the realms stretching away around him. From his vantage point and god eyes he could see all nine worlds that were held within the branches of Yggdrasil, the tree of life, each one holding secrets of the beings who lived there. Midgard, the home of the humans, lay below him, decay visible around the edges. If something wasn't done soon the gods and goddesses would disappear forever, their myths and legends fading into the mists of time to be forgotten.

He began to walk, his measured steps leading him toward the castle where Odin, the ruler of the Aesir, lived. He'd never been here, but he knew the place, and knew of the gods and goddesses who reigned here. The gate opened at his touch and he walked through into the castle keep, focusing on the massive entrance one hundred feet away. He had a story to tell.

11

K at headed to work hoping that Gwen would show up. She'd been gone for two weeks now and Kat had not gotten her paycheck. If she didn't get money today, she would have to raid the till to pay her rent. For some reason the dog had insisted on coming along, whining and barking when she attempted to leave without her. She had finally given in, worried that if she continued barking while Kat was at work her neighbors would complain and she could get ousted. And right now, she couldn't deal with any more uncertainty in her life.

Her mind went to Brant as she walked the two miles to work, the dog heeling by her side. She found herself checking down dark alleys, and looking for him among the homeless who leaned against walls or lay sleeping under dirty sleeping bags, but there was no sign of him. A crazy man ran up to her, his eyes glazed as he shouted that the world was coming to an end. She side-stepped around him and kept going, doom settling into her from his prophetic words. In the distance she heard sirens, the sound of them giving her a sense of urgency. She hurried on.

Once she reached the shop, she was relieved to find the door open and Gwen on a stool hunched over the desk wearing half glasses. She looked up and stuffed some papers in the drawer and locked it. "Sorry for my absence, dear," she said, rising to embrace Kat. "Several things have happened recently that took all my attention."

"Is your daughter okay?"

"My daughter?" She looked blank before her eyes brightened. "Oh, yes, she's fine. She had a small accident and I needed to take care of her for a few days. I should have called, but…"

"It's all right," Kat interrupted. "But I do need to get paid today."

"Oh, my goodness! I forgot completely!" She reached into the register and counted out the cash and handed it over.

"Thanks. Have you heard from Brant's mother?" Kat asked as she stuffed the cash into her bag and hung it on the coat rack.

Gwen frowned, an expression of confusion passing across her features. "Um, no. Sadly I haven't had the time."

"So, Brant could be anywhere right now."

"I told you before that I'm sure he's fine," Gwen said crisply. "He's a smart boy."

Kat wondered how a twelve-year-old boy living among drug addicts could be fine, but she'd didn't argue. Sadness moved through her, followed by a vision of a raven, its head pressed into her palm.

"Did you find some herbs while I've been gone? Our supply is running low," Gwen asked in a business-like tone.

Kat looked at the dog staring up at her as though waiting

for her answer. "The woods where I usually go…it's hard to explain. It could have been my imagination, but it…it didn't really have any color. And I felt…"

Gwen's head shot up from where she was examining the pile of mail. "What? What are you saying?"

Kat shrugged, surprised by the woman's reaction. "The forest looked like a black and white photograph, or maybe more like a blurry over-exposed grayed out-photo. There was an energy that didn't feel right." She let out a nervous laugh. I'm sure I imagined it."

Gwen stared at her for a full minute without speaking, her eyes like saucers. When she finally spoke, her words were halting. "Do not go there again, Kat. Have you seen that man?"

"You mean the one who…?"

"Yes," she answered impatiently.

"Not lately."

"Are you having visions?"

"A few, I guess. I had a weird dream, plus that vision of the forest…"

"That wasn't a vision, Kat. There *is* a dangerous energy that has come into this world. Tell me about your dream."

Dangerous energy that has come in…? "It was about a raven—that's all. And a guy came to wash my windows and kind of scared me."

"A guy—what guy? Was this part of your dream?"

Why was Gwen getting so worked up? "No, this was real. He said his name was Jones. He gave me his business card. He was carrying a gun."

"A window washer carrying a gun," she mused, staring at the floor. "What did Pooka do?"

What did that have to do with anything? "She growled."

Gwen glanced at the dog. "Good girl," she muttered. "Anything else odd—memories that don't seem like part of your life, or…?"

"You are more than you think you are," Kat intoned. "You need to remember."

"Where did you hear that?"

Kat laughed. "I imagined a ghost in the forest—she said it."

"A ghost? What did this ghost look like?"

"A woman? I don't know—she was too wispy to make out."

Gwen stood and took hold of Kat's upper arm, her fingers digging in painfully. "You need to take these things seriously. They are messages from beyond and are meant to steer you toward your destiny."

"What? What destiny?" she scoffed, pulling out of the older woman's vice- like grasp.

"I'm serious. You have no idea of the peril…" She stopped in mid-sentence, her eyes going opaque. "I want you to meditate and take heed of whatever comes up."

"I can't—it's too creepy."

"Creepy?"

"The last time I meditated all I saw was burnt trees and everything was like dead."

Gwen frowned. "I agree with your ghost. You need to remember. It will either come upon you unawares and scare you, or it will arrive as visions do, during your meditation."

"Why are you being so weird?" Kat asked, trying to shake the dread the woman evoked in her.

Gwen shook her head, turning away. "I'm a seer, a psychic."

"Since when?"

"Since always."

At that moment the bell jingled, and their first customer walked into the shop.

On her way home that afternoon Kat's thoughts were scattered and wild, several odd visions appearing in her mind. In one of them Brant was grown, his head bending to hers just before he kissed her. She let out a shriek and backed away, but there was no one in front of her, aside from a few pedestrians walking along the sidewalk and talking on their phones.

A few minutes later she was listening to the grown-up version of Brant tell her that she was half goddess. She laughed shakily and tried to shake his earnest expression from her mind, but it persisted. Her body trembled as she saw him naked and hovering over her... "Oh my **god!**" Several people turned to stare at her when her shout rang out, her face flushing, her entire body drenched in a sudden sweat. Pooka moved close, her amber eyes taking in Kat's distress. She let out a bark. "Did you see it too?" she whispered. She could swear the damn dog smiled before pulling against the leash to hurry her along.

When she reached the apartment, she immediately went to take a shower, hoping to quell the sexual feelings that continued to surge through her. But the water didn't help, more images tumbling through her mind to drive her nearly crazy with a longing she couldn't explain. A half goddess? She tried to laugh but the words swirled around her, taunting her and refusing to let go.

In her bedroom her gaze lit on her Celtic knot pendant

lying on the dresser, the memory of older Brant wearing a nearly identical one floating through her mind. He had told her that they were destined to meet. But other memories seemed to conflict with that one, scenes taking on a life of their own as she was shuttled through time without being able to determine which had come first. After wrestling with the visions, she finally fell into bed, her mind shutting down as she closed her eyes.

His name is Bran, she heard herself say as she woke up in the morning. An image of raven went through her mind, as if they were one in the same. Brant and Bran—were *they* the same person? How could they be? Brant was only twelve years old. She felt wrung out, her mind blown by the visions, and what seemed to be memories from a completely impossible past. Her cell phone ran, startling her. It was Gwen—the first time she'd ever had a call from the older woman.

"Are you all right?"

"Are your psychic abilities telling you I'm not?"

"Please just answer the question."

"Not really. I had the strange thought that Brant is also this man named Bran, who apparently, I was in love with."

"What else have you realized?"

"Realized or imagined?"

"Kat, please take this seriously. I'm trying to determine if you're ready for what I have to say."

Without going into lurid detail Kat went through the oddness of the evening before as she recounted the mixed-up memories that made no sense.

When she was finished Gwen said, "It's time for us to have a long talk. Can you meet me at the coffee shop before work?"

Dagda gazed down at Siobhan as she slept, his heart filling until it felt like it might burst. The act of giving birth had done more than bring their baby into the world, it had also infused her with the past, her memories from their previous life intact. It seemed impossible, and yet she knew—had always known who he was. Her cheeks had filled in during the past two months of bedrest, her shoulder blades no longer jutting. Mior gazed up at Dagda, his dark eyes knowing. Was it normal for a baby to be so *aware?*

"What are you doing, Dag?"

His gaze shifted to Siobhan, nervous fingers running through his dark curls. "Mior, he's quite something, isn't he?"

Siobhan smiled, pushing herself up to sitting. "He's the miracle that his name says he is."

Dagda had a moment of disquiet, a feeling that he had pushed the limit of his luck. Things were too wonderful, too perfect.

"Why are you frowning, you silly man? Come here," she invited, pulling him into her arms.

He felt her softness and fragility, tears squeezing out of the corners of his eyes as he buried his face in her hair, the scents of vanilla and lemon permeating his senses. "I love you so much," he murmured, his desire for her making itself known. But when the baby began a mewling cry he pulled away, watching her slide the nightgown off her shoulder and place Mior at her breast.

"It won't be long now," she said, smiling at him as the baby suckled.

"I…"

"I know you, Dag. I've known you through basically two lifetimes now. Don't try and pretend this isn't on your mind."

"What about you, Siobhan? Do you think about it?"

"Of course. Now be a saint and fix me a cup of fennel and fenugreek tea. I fear that this fast-growing boy is taxing my ability to produce enough milk."

Dagda's expression changed to one of confusion. "He…needs more than you're making?"

Siobhan laughed. "You are such a worrywart. Shoo now," she said, waving her hand in the air.

Dagda left the room, emotions sending his thoughts careening into places he didn't want to go. Back at the castle he'd put off Siobhan's questions about Kat, citing the need to get her home and into her own bed. Over the months they'd been home he'd managed to avoid the topic every time she brought it up, either changing the subject or using the excuse of being on his way to work—not that he went to the office that often anymore. It was a full-time job preparing food for her, helping her bathe and making sure her health was actually improving. The roses had come back into her cheeks, her eyes sparkling as they had before... *before she died the second time*, he thought grimly.

She knew when he was lying, just as she knew that controlling his sexual desire was becoming more difficult. Frigg had warned him, told him that Siobhan needed time to heal. His gaze went into the garden where the wisteria still held on to purple blooms. Siobhan was like a beautiful flower, one that needed careful tending. A smile curled up the corners of his wide mouth. He'd never known anyone like Siobhan, her ability to see right through him unnerving as well as utterly beguiling. Her questions wouldn't stop until she knew the truth.

Later, after he'd placed Mior in his basket and climbed into bed beside her, he realized that it was nearly time to visit Frigg and Freya. Would they have good news regarding her health, or would he have to wait interminably? An image of Morrighan flitted through his mind, her luscious, overripe body affecting him more than he expected. He pushed the image away and reached for Siobhan, pulling her close. She sighed in her sleep, snuggling into him and making things worse. He finally rose from bed and went to take a cold shower.

13

"Your father is Dagda, the all-father god, who has broken every rule there is. He is living with your mother, who he has resurrected from the dead, and now no one can locate him. He's been taking your memories, Kat. He's the one you've seen in the forest. You are a half goddess with powers that have not been allowed to unfold."

The woman had already explained her own role, that she was Cerridwen, the crone goddess of inspiration, who had originally been sent by Dagda to look after Kat. "But why would he send you to protect me and then do what he's done?"

"Apparently your mother's resurrection was a spur of the moment decision. After that was completed, he realized that he couldn't allow you to remember."

"Because...?"

"Because you might disapprove, which could lead to all sorts of complications."

As Gwen talked on, flickering lights shimmered around Kat, her mind a tumble of muddled thoughts and images. She didn't know if it was today, yesterday, or tomorrow, her sense of time and place gone as she struggled in a turbulent sea. When Gwen stopped for a moment, Kat was suddenly aware that the two of them were sitting in a private corner of the coffee shop, the high booth hiding them from other patrons. The last sentence Gwen had spoken rang in her ears. *His latest treachery has summoned dark energies that could lead to the end of the world.*

Kat's gaze met Gwen's. "How can that be? He's only one person."

"He's a god, Kat. God's are not allowed to do what he is doing. He's upset the balance and created a rupture in the web that holds everything in place."

"What *is* he doing?"

Gwen let out a long sigh before she glanced over her shoulder. She leaned forward. "I thought I explained all that. He has resurrected your mother and is living somewhere on earth with her."

"I knew that…but…" Kat's mouth dropped open as the memories of meeting her father rushed unbidden into her mind. "I remember now…he…he asked me if I wanted to keep my memories. I told him yes. And then…"

"And then he took them. He wants to block your powers. He's afraid of who you are."

"My powers?" She shook her head. "I don't have any powers."

"Didn't you say you remembered Bran and what he told you? You experienced something magical with him, did you not?"

"Bran…" She looked up. Is Brant Bran?"

Gwen nodded.

"So that's why you weren't worried about him—why did

he do that—I mean come and live with me as a twelve-year-old?"

"Bran is a god of protection. He had to keep Dagda from using his magic to take away your memories."

Kat stared blankly into the distance. "So that I..."

"So that you'd remember him and also re-discover who you are."

"Where's Bran now?"

Gwen shook her head, her eyes going dark. "He's gone."

Gone. The word conjured bleak emptiness. A feeling of loss settled into her. "He left because of Cedar."

"Not only Cedar. He was in terrible emotional pain being with you that way. He lost hope."

Kat began to cry, her body twisting in the seat as the realizations poured in. She loved Bran but he was gone. Her mother was alive but Kat didn't know where she was. Her life was in shambles, the past like a road that had been torn apart and covered over with fast growing vines, her future as uncertain as the clouds massing in the distance. "What am I going to do?" she whispered, gazing at Gwen through her tears.

Gwen reached across the table and took hold of her hand. "First you're going to uncover who you are. And then...we will see."

Pooka let out a bark from where Kat had tied her outside the coffee shop. Gwen placed some money on the table and tugged her up. "Pooka's restless."

"Poor doggie," Kat said, rising her feet.

"Pooka is no simple dog, Kat. She's a protection spirit."

Kat stared at Gwen before hurrying toward the door,

her gaze on the dog whose eyes had turned gold. She untied her and placed a hand on her soft head, her eyes swimming with tears. "Why did he leave?" she whispered, a band tightening around her chest.

"I can't work right now," Kat said as she and Gwen walked together to the shop.

Gwen nodded. "We'll close it up for today. Tell me again what you saw in the forest?"

Kat let out a breath. "It was gray instead of green. And I felt...weird energies, like spiders crawling on me."

"Your powers are definitely returning. Now we have to make sure Dagda doesn't find you again."

"Pooka chased him away the last time."

Gwen smiled, reaching for the key inside her purse when they arrived at the shop. "Let's continue talking in the back room."

Once they were settled and Pooka had a bowl of water and a few biscuits in her bowl, Kat asked, "How do I do this...I mean turn into a goddess?"

Gwen laughed. "You don't have to turn into one—you are one. Now that it's begun, it shouldn't take long. I have the sense that your destiny is connected with this dark turn of events."

"What do you mean?"

Gwen gazed out the window. "I don't have the gift of prophecy. Perhaps we should seek out someone who does." She turned to face Kat again. "But now is not the time for that."

Kat wondered when the right time would be. If the forest was turning gray and dark energies were rising up, wasn't it time to act? "I want Bran to come back," she muttered as his adult face appeared in her mind.

Gwen frowned. "I do too, but from what Airmid told me, he could be gone a very long time."

"Airmid!" Kat fell back against the chair as memories of her apartment with the tree crowded into her mind. "She...she was really mean to Bran."

"It is forbidden for gods to be with humans. She didn't know you were a goddess."

"And Bran did?"

"I'm not sure if he knew by then—he tried very hard to stay away from you, but..."

Kat nodded, tears welling. "We loved each other and now he's given up on me."

Gwen gazed at her sadly.

It was early evening before Kat left the shop, Pooka next to her as she waved goodbye to Gwen standing in the doorway. The sky had turned mauve with streaks of orange, the long summer twilight beginning. "I promise I'll be here tomorrow!" she called out, watching Gwen smile and close the door.

As she walked the empty streets toward home, each new memory vied for prominence, confusing her with differing timelines that made no sense; small snippets of conversation complicated things further as she attempted to place them in logical order. She remembered the time *before* Dagda, meeting Bran and living in Airmid's apartment and helping with the pop-ups to sell her herbal concoctions. She also remembered

Rhiannon and the jealousy she felt regarding the gorgeous woman's relationship with Bran. It all seemed so trivial now in the face of what she'd recalled.

The memory of Bran's incredible wall-free apartment entered her mind—with his help she'd realized who she was. That was where they'd made love in the real world for the first time. Her mind clung to those memories, her body remembering every amazing sensation. Her eyes filled thinking about him, and knowing the pain he must be going through. Or maybe he'd decided it wasn't worth the effort and had turned his back on her.

She was on a side street when she noticed a man walking toward her. It was mere seconds later that he pulled out a gun and pointed it at her. She was paralyzed for a moment, and in that few seconds he pulled the trigger, the bullet headed straight for Pooka. Kat watched the bullet's trajectory, lost inside a slow-downed version of time; she heard the hiss as it moved through the air. When she glanced at the dog, all she saw was a shimmer of movement as the bullet moved past them and hit a telephone pole. The man, who she now recognized as Jones, stared at them wide-eyed and then pointed again, but before he could discharge the weapon Kat and Pooka rushed past him.

When time returned to normal, she was standing in front of her apartment. "Did you do that?" she asked, fishing in her bag for her key with shaking hands. Inside she bolted the door and fell onto the couch, trembling all over. Her question went unanswered as Pooka jumped up and curled up next to her. But something told her that it wasn't the dog who altered time—it was her.

"What did you just say?" Dagda's eyes turned dark as the sea during a storm, his expression rigid as he stared at Jones.

"I'm sorry, but she…I don't know how to explain it, sir. One minute she was there and in the next she was gone."

"The dog too?"

"Both of them."

"Goddamn it," Dagda muttered, staring down at his desk.

"What do you want me to do?"

Dagda looked up. "Nothing for the moment. I have to think." He waved him away.

This was the first time he'd been here in three weeks, and he was not pleased with what Jones had just told him. Kat's powers were coming on. On top of this news he was fielding Siobhan's questions regarding Kat and trying to maintain an expression of innocence. If she kept going, he knew he would break down. Siobhan had always had that effect on him.

But how was he to deal with this situation? If Kat had

her powers it was only a matter of time before she found him. He knew it like he knew his own mind. "Fuck!" he roared, the windows rattling with the force of his bellow.

The door opened, Beatrice's face appearing. "Is everything all right, sir?"

"Everything is not all right, Beatrice, but I'm dealing with it."

She nodded and disappeared, the door closing softly behind her.

At home later when he faced his wife new worries sprang up.

"Mior needs something I don't have," Siobhan told him, gazing down at the wailing baby.

"What do you mean? Milk isn't enough?"

"He's his father's son, Dag, and I'm human."

"We didn't have this problem with Katel." He realized his mistake the second the words tumbled out of his mouth. He braced himself for her questions, but all she said was, "Every child is different."

Dagda frowned and picked up the baby whose face was bright red from crying. "What is it?" he asked. The baby stopped crying to stare at him, his eyes so dark they looked nearly black. A message was transmitted, what the baby needed clear in Dagda's mind. He turned to Siobhan. "We have to go back to the castle as soon as possible. I need to talk this over with Freya and Frigg. Are you up to it?"

Siobhan nodded, worry lines crisscrossing her forehead. "When?"

When he placed the baby at her breast, Mior turned his head away, a thin wail shattering the quiet. His gaze met Siobhan's, tandem expressions of panic on both their faces. "Tonight."

Odin met them at the front door his expression filled with fury. "Bran ap Llyr was just here and has told me of your treachery. I knew some of this already, but I was not aware of the lengths you've gone to in order to achieve your selfish desires, or about the ones you've hurt along the way, including your daughter. If you do not make amends for your actions I will be forced to get involved. In order to bring the balance back you must return to Otherworld and take your punishment."

Siobhan shook with terror, her hand on his arm to steady herself as Dagda faced the one-eyed god. He glanced at her, guilt taking his breath. "I cannot leave Siobhan," Dadga mumbled.

Odin glanced at Siobhan and the baby in her arms. "Bringing this woman into your treachery will cost her, Dagda, and your son as well. No act that is against the laws of nature goes unpaid. You will come to justice." He stared at Dagda for another moment before turning to stride off, his imposing figure lost as he rounded the castle wall.

Once Odin was gone, Dagda put his arm around Siobhan's waist to help her inside and toward the bedroom where Frigg and Freya waited. But instead of moving she stood rooted, her worried gaze going to his face. "What was he talking about? What have you done to Katel?"

"Not now, Siobhan. Our son needs the skills of Frigg and Freya," he muttered before dragging her down the long hallway. The baby lay nestled in her arms asleep, but the jostling woke him, a piercing shriek coming from his mouth just as they entered the room.

Frigg and Freya turned from the window, their swirling eyes focusing on the baby. Frigg hurried over and took Mior out of Siobhan's arms, soothing him with a magical wave. Freya gave Dagda a dark look before helping Siobhan into bed, her soft murmurs soothing the distraught woman. As Frigg rocked Mior, Dagda paced, his restlessness growing by the minute. "The baby needs..."

"Yes, Dagda, we can both see what he needs. He is a god's son and needs the milk of a goddess to supplement his growing appetite. He grows very quickly," she murmured, looking down at Mior in her arms. "He will be built like his father."

A swell of pride moved through Dagda until he glanced at Siobhan who stared at him with narrowed eyes. He turned to Frigg, trying to hide the uneasy feeling that came over him. "Is there a goddess here, who...?"

"Both Freya and I are capable of feeding him. But that will require him to stay."

Siobhan made a little sound, tears sliding down her cheeks. "I can't leave him here. Can I feed him too?"

Frigg smiled, turning to Siobhan. "Of course. You're his mother—he needs your milk. We will merely supplement with ours. It is not a matter of calories, it is a matter of magic, something as a human woman you cannot supply."

Siobhan relaxed back against the pillows. "Will I stay here then?"

Frigg glanced at Dagda. "Will you stay or go, Dagda?"

Dagda turned, trying to bring his focus back to the

matter at hand. "I…I have a business to run, and…how long will this need to go on?"

"Until he is old enough to take solid food. So at least two moons." Freya turned to Siobhan. "And we will need to examine you to make sure your healing is going as it should."

Siobhan smiled wanly until the baby began to wail, her gaze going helplessly to Frigg who had already exposed her breast, cooing to him as she placed her nipple in his mouth. Siobhan turned away from the scene, wiping at her tears. "I feel so useless," she muttered.

Frigg sat on the bed, cradling the baby close as he suckled. "It isn't a matter of being useless, Siobhan. He is, after all, a god's son. You must try and understand."

Dagda's gaze went to Frigg's milk-white breast, the contrast of the baby's dark head against her translucent skin. He sucked in his breath, visualizing his mouth where Mior's was, his fingers tangled in that silken mane of hair, a raw wave of desire surging through his body. He tried to look away, but he was transfixed, unable to do anything but stare, his manhood pressing against his trousers. *Gods, what in hell is wrong with me?*

When he glanced at Siobhan she gestured for him to come close and took his hand in hers. "It's all right," she whispered in his ear. "It's been a long time."

He buried his face in her hair, tears welling. "It's you I want."

"Come back in a week, Dagda," Freya told him after the baby had been sated and plans had been made. "By then we will have more news regarding Mior, as well as your wife."

Mior was now snuggled against Siobhan, his face rosy as he slept. "We will figure out a daily schedule," he heard Frigg telling Siobhan. "Perhaps an early morning feed and one before bed might suffice. During the day he will be all yours."

Dagda's heart constricted with longing. "I hate to leave you."

"You would go crazy if you stayed."

He nodded, knowing she was right.

"But when you get back, I expect a full accounting about Katel."

Dagda felt a sudden dread, wondering what he would tell her. He'd have to come up with a very good lie in order for her to believe him.

"I mean it, Dag," she said sharply, the two goddesses turning to her in surprise.

He nodded and came close, touching his lips to hers briefly before straightening. Without another word he was out of the room and striding down the hall toward the entrance, several disturbing emotions worming their evil way into his mind.

15

"This is wonderful news!" Gwen gushed when Kat told her about the bullet and the time distortion. They were in the shop together as rain poured down from a slate-colored sky. A rumble of thunder could be heard in the distance.

"Wonderful that this man wants to kill Pooka and maybe me as well?"

Gwen made a grimace. "You know what I mean—your powers are returning."

"I have no memory of being able to slow time down."

"Perhaps you didn't back then. It was early days when he took your memories the first time. You're twenty-two now, with more abilities arriving with each passing day. It is high time you understand what you're capable of."

"I have the sense that these things only happen when I'm stressed. I didn't control it, Gwen."

"That may be true, but as the abilities grow, you will begin to understand how to command them." The older woman turned from wrapping a phone order. "What of other memories?"

Kat let out a sigh, her gaze going to the corners where dust bunnies lay in wait for when the door opened and they could skitter to other hiding places. It was late summer now and the air was heavy with humidity and heat, the rain making it worse. Vacuuming was needed, dusting as well. "I don't really know. I've had muddled thoughts and visions about a pond and goddesses, and…you…Bran was there too."

Gwen nodded. "That's the intersection between earth and Otherworld. I doubt you would find much there now."

"What do you mean? It's a dreamscape."

"It's a dreamscape *and* Otherworld, Kat. And with what's going on I assume it would be similar to what you found in the forest."

Kat felt a pang. "But…that's where my dreams always took me—how can it…?"

"You've been visiting Otherworld for years without even knowing it. I am sorry that it is no longer a place of solace for you."

"What do I do now? I can barely keep my mind on work or customers or anything. And now that I remember him, I miss Bran so much. And what about my mom? Will she know me?"

Gwen shook her head. "She will have no memory of you or her former life. And as far as finding her, six gods have been searching and haven't been able to discover where Dagda is hiding."

"He uses protection spells and magic to keep them out," Kat muttered.

"Just so. As far as work, I suggest you do this job while you're in the early stages of this. It wouldn't do to have you wandering around without understanding what you're capable of."

"I figure my father sent Jones, but why he wants to kill Pooka eludes me."

"Pooka is keeping you safe from Dagda, who wants to keep taking your memories. And if he gets away with it, as he's been doing this past year, you'll never discover who you are."

Kat made a face and turned to stare out the door at the haze of rain. A flash of lightning lit up the sky. Mosquitos buzzed around the screen, trying to get inside. "I'm not sure I want to be who I'm supposed to be. It seems like I'll have some momentous job to do that will be all-consuming and that I'm not prepared for."

"The job has to be about saving…"

"The world?" She let out a mirthless laugh. "That's exactly what I'm talking about."

"I was going to say saving Otherworld from being destroyed. And that will only require taking the Dagda back to stand trial."

"How long has he been at this? You think *I* can find him when no one else can? Life was way simpler when I was living with Bran, and we were…" Tears welled as she envisioned him, his loving mossy eyes on hers. He was handsome and funny and oh so good in bed. *Amazing*, in fact. "Will Bran ever come back?"

Gwen pursed her lips and placed two neatly wrapped packages on the counter. "I couldn't say. According to Airmid he was desolate when she talked with him. It may take some time for him to process what happened and come back to himself."

"As a god, right? Meanwhile what am I supposed to do? After what I remember about him, and how we were together, no one else will do."

Gwen chortled. "A god can definitely have that effect on you."

"Speaking of gods, what was with you and that guy...the lawyer, Forsetti?"

Gwen colored. "He's the god of justice—what else do you want to know?"

"I know *that*. Are you, or were you lovers?"

Gwen turned away for a second, trying to hide her reddening face. "Yes, we were once very close."

"I thought you were way older than him, but I guess in god and goddess time how many wrinkles you have doesn't count."

"Our appearance is often an illusion. One of these days you will know this from personal experience."

The bell rang and the door opened and two stout women wearing loose fitting linen capris and holding umbrellas entered. One of them was there to pick up the packages on the counter, but the other needed help. Kat rose reluctantly from her chair and went to assist her.

After the customers were gone Gwen caught Kat's gaze, the older woman's expression serious. "I think we need Airmid to help you through this, Kat. I am too old and she is more versed in such things."

"Such things—like latent powers suddenly taking me over? I hope that doesn't happen."

"With Airmid's tutelage it won't. Would you be willing to entrust yourself to her?"

Kat thought for a second, remembering. "I don't know...she was..."

"So you've said, but she was only trying to obey our

rules—no fraternization between gods and humans."

Questions crowded like vultures demanding answers.
"Are you…immortal?"

"Well, yes, I suppose. But we *can* die."

"Are you all ugly and old, but look young? Not you, of
course, but…"

Gwen laughed. "Because I *am* ugly and old?"

"I didn't mean it like that!" Kat cried out, a flush of heat
rising into her cheeks. "I just meant…"

Gwen held up her hand. "We do sometimes use a
glamour to change our appearance, like Bran appearing as
a twelve-year-old boy, but I am the keeper of the cauldron
of knowledge, inspiration and rebirth. If you look closer
you will see that I am not as ancient as you at first thought.
As far as Bran, in his true state he is one of the most
handsome of all the gods."

Kat saw him in her mind's eye wearing the tunic and
loose pants, his hair clean and tied back. A tingle of want
moved through her, stopping her breath for a second.

"You might not know it, but I have given you the elixir
from my cauldron of rebirth, hoping to encourage your
memories."

"Tea?"

"Yes."

"Do you really have a daughter?"

Gwen glanced down at the floor. "No."

"I thought not, since I've never met her in all the time
I've worked here."

"My sister goddess's and I represent the divine
feminine, Kat. Do you know what that means?"

"The divine feminine…not really."

"Instead of going along with the current male dominated thought, we honor who we are as women. In Otherworld there is no hierarchy between god and goddess. We are all powerful in our own ways and learn from each other."

"I like the sound of that."

"Now, my dear—what have you concluded regarding Airmid?"

"I guess I forgive her," she said hesitantly. "And I do need mentoring."

"Good. As far as the shop goes, I've just changed my mind. Distracting yourself with work will not encourage that process. I'm here now and you can relieve me when you wish. It is not as though I need the money."

"You don't need the money?"

"Of course not. I'm a goddess—I have magic at my fingertips."

"When will I meet with Airmid?"

"As soon as I contact her."

"What about my rent? I won't have the money to pay it."

"It will be taken care of," Gwen said, winking.

Kat was glad when she reached the apartment, part of her on the constant look-out for Jones or some other minion sent by her father. The rain had stopped for the time being, but dark storm clouds loomed, the low rumble of thunder in the distance. Why was her father doing this to her? It made no sense. He'd been so sweet when they met, asking her questions and then moved to tears. She remembered him in her apartment, his enormous bulk taking up the entire couch, how he ran his fingers through his unruly curls, and the way he stared at her with his head cocked as though memorizing her features. Why would he want to block the goddess side of her, keep her from knowing her full potential? And why would he stay away from Otherworld knowing that that alone was causing the destruction of his homeland? None of it made any sense to her. What she'd seen of him just didn't support that level of selfishness. But then again, she'd only met him twice. Maybe bringing her mom back from the dead had done something to his good sense.

Pooka gave bark, bringing her mind back to the present. She reached in her bag for the key, stuck it in the lock and turned it, swinging the door open as her mind switched gears to Airmid and what the process with her would look like. Because of her distraction she didn't notice the dark figure inside the apartment until it was too late, a gunshot splitting the silence. Pooka dropped, her body turning to dust as a tiny spark lifted into the air. It hovered for a few seconds before it disappeared upward. Kat was too stunned to even notice the noxious smoke, or the man wearing a gas mask. She choked, her throat raw as her world dimmed and went dark.

Kat woke to utter darkness. She was hot, her body aching and bruised. As her eyes adjusted, she noticed a thin line of light above her...maybe a trap door? Her fingers touched dirt, an earthy and chemical smell in the air. She must be in a basement, but whose basement and where, she had no idea. Her throat constricted as she thought of the terrible moment when the dog was no more. But whatever spirit resided inside that dog was still alive—she'd seen it. Her head felt as though someone had pounded it with a mallet.

Shaky, she pushed herself up to explore her prison, working her way slowly around the packed earth edges to determine its size. By the end of her slow turning she estimated it to be around ten feet by ten feet, and as far as she could tell, the only way in or out was through the trapdoor in the ceiling.

She was dozing when she heard the squeak of the trap door opening. She stood too quickly, putting a hand out to steady herself before blinking in the light. "Who's there?" she called out. "What do you want with me?"

A backlit figure leaned over the opening, a package thudding onto the ground before the trapdoor was lowered again. "Wait! Who are you?" There was no answer as footsteps receded, the sound of a door closing before she was once more left in silence. She crawled along the floor and felt for the package, her fingernails scraping through the dirt. It was larger than she'd expected, a cardboard box tied with string. Inside she found a battery powered Coleman lantern, a bottle of water and a sandwich. At least they wanted her to live. *And to see,* she thought, switching the lamp on. The space was nearly round, some rocks visible here and there, as though it had been dug long ago as a root cellar or cold storage for something. *Or a prison in which to hold someone indefinitely,* a little voice in her head added. The sandwich was tuna with too much mayo, but she ate it anyway, chugging two thirds of the water to wash it down. Less than an hour later her belly began to rumble and she realized there was no place to do her business.

By the time the trapdoor opened again, (whether hours or days, she didn't know), the space had begun to stink, her insides continuing to rebel against the tuna. She'd dug a hole and covered it, but the stench persisted. Another package was thrown down, her shouts ignored as the door was dropped into place—another sandwich and a bottle of water, which she opened immediately, guzzling the liquid down. When she saw another tuna sandwich, a spasm had her doubling up. She barely had time to pull her pants down and squat.

Afterward she lay on the floor, exhausted and sick. She had no idea if it was day or night, her entire world narrowed down to this room. "What do you want with me?" she shouted weakly. But there was no one there.

She was sure days had gone by, her throat hoarse from screaming and crying, when she detected voices in the room above. "How long has she been here?"

"A week, sir."

"Jesus, Jones! I told you I'd be gone for a while. This is inhumane!"

"I fed and watered her—she's fine."

"She's not a fucking animal," the second man growled. "And from the smell I'd say she isn't fine at all."

"Sorry—forgot to add a poop bucket, and then it was too late."

It was only another moment before the trapdoor

opened, something hissing downward to land on the ground next to her. Kat stared at the reddish object emitting a grayish gas as she attempted to place the voice. But by the time she determined who the voice belonged to, she was already losing consciousness.

Dagda stared at his unconscious daughter, conflicting emotions making his head pound. She lay on the couch in his office, her pale face just as he remembered it. He could see himself in her features, but mostly she resembled Siobhan, with her chestnut hair and high cheekbones. He let out a long sigh and began to pace, his fingers clenching and unclenching. He knew what he had to do, but putting her through that ordeal had already made her sick. Was it wise to take her memories when she was in this weakened condition?

His thoughts went to Siobhan. It had been weeks since he left her at Odin's castle. When he'd returned from dropping her and the baby off, his commercial real estate business had claimed him, taking him into other countries in order to conceal what was beginning to come to light; if his creditors found out how he was financing things he would go to jail; gun-running and smuggling drugs were a big no-no. And along the way he'd discovered that some of the people he counted on were not as loyal as he'd hoped. A few had needed to be culled. An ugly job but someone had to do it. Humans were easily swayed to greed, their common sense disappearing as they attempted to line their own pockets. As a god it was easy to detect.

He glanced at his daughter again. She had to wake up in order for his magic to work. As soon as that was completed, he would drug her again and send her off with Jones. Once back in her apartment she would be blissfully unaware of everything she'd remembered these past weeks. He chuckled, thinking about Cerridwen and Airmid's reactions when they found they were back to square one. After spying on them Jones had reported what they had in mind for her, the mentoring to help her understand and control her goddess powers. But when he asked Dagda what it all meant, Dagda had waved a hand in front of his face making him forget he'd ever heard it.

In the next moment he was thinking about Siobhan and her insistence that he tell her what was going on with Kat. How could he tell her he'd drugged their daughter and taken her memories?

"Dad?"

He swung around to see Kat pushing herself up to sitting.

"Are you responsible me being in that disgusting cellar for who knows how long?"

Dadga hung his head, trying to push back his guilt. "I had to, Kat. You were..."

"Where's Mom? I want to see her."

Dagda crossed the room to hover over her. "She's recovering from childbirth."

"Child...isn't she a little old for that?"

"I made her young."

Kat let out a sigh, rubbing at her head. "Did the baby survive?"

"Of course he did—what do you take me for?"

"A boy then—what's his name?"

"Enough of this, Katel. I can't let you remember any of this—it's too dangerous for me."

"Oh, so that's what you're doing. I won't tell anybody."

"You may say that now, but when push comes to shove…"

"You're afraid of me, of what I am. I know what you've done and I also know that it's affecting your homeland. Don't you care about that?"

Dagda frowned, running agitated fingers through his thick curls. "You want me to leave your mother and your baby brother and go to Otherworld to be imprisoned?"

"Take them with you."

"It's forbidden!" he roared.

Kat had placed her feet on the floor, preparing to stand, when he pushed her back. "I cannot let you loose on the world. I'm sorry." He held her gaze, his eyes swirling as he moved his hands in the intricate movements.

Kat fell back, her eyes widening.

When Dagda blew out a breath, enveloping her in a fine mist, her eyes closed and she slumped sideways. "Jones!" he shouted.

The door opened. "Yes, sir?"

"Take her back to her apartment. The plane is waiting. And if she wakes up, dose her again. She needs to forget everything."

"Dose her—with the gas in the canisters?"

"Yes, and do it before she comes completely around. I

don't want her having a memory of this meeting, or of you."

"Yes, sir." Jones went to the couch and lifted her into his arms. A moment later Dagda shut the office door behind him, guilt and shame swirling through him as he contemplated what he'd just done. It was time to go to Siobhan, and probably time to bring her home, but the idea of discussing Katel with her had him quaking in his boots.

"Where are Siobhan and Mior?" Dagda asked, staring into the empty bedroom. The bed was made and no clothing was hung over chairs, not even a glass remained on the nightstand. The late afternoon sunlight sifted through the open window, the aroma of dried leaves wafting in with it. It was fall now, the days growing shorter, the nights growing long.

Frigg turned from where she was gazing out the window. Her lace-up bodice had been loosened, both breasts exposed to show the baby in her arms contentedly suckling.

Dagda swallowed, trying not to focus on her breasts or the silken hair that hung over one shoulder and tickled Mior's cheek. When she smiled something inside of him gave way, as though his pent-up lust would explode if he didn't do something about it instantly.

Frigg leaned down to place the baby in his basket, the firm roundness of her breasts holding his gaze. When she straightened and reached to do up her bodice, Dagda crossed the room in two strides, stilling her hand. He gazed at her, his fingers tracing lazy circles around her nipple. "So lush and beautiful," he murmured, pressing his mouth there. When she didn't resist, he gripped the fabric of her gown and pushed it up around her hips, feasting his eyes on her nakedness as he lifted her and pressed her back against the wall. He kissed her as he fumbled with his trousers, unable to wait. A second later he was deep inside her, his rough thrusting movements making her cry out. But when he gazed into her eyes, he could see it was pleasure, not pain, that had caused it.

As they reached the pinnacle, she arched against him, her legs tight around his waist as he finished. When it was over, he carried her to the bed and placed her down, helping her lace up her gown as he tried to gauge her reaction. "I'm sorry, Frigg, I…"

She smiled up at him. "If you had done to your wife what you just did to me, you would have killed her. I'm glad I was here."

Dagda stared at her. "You planned this?"

"Yes, Dagda, I saw how you looked at me the last time. With your history I knew this would happen. And it's a good thing. Your wife is human and fragile. You must be careful with her."

Dagda smiled. "Thank you. And please, do not mention this to Odin."

Frigg laughed. "Odin and I are companions, not lovers. He would not be happy to hear about my giving myself to *you*, in particular, but we live our own lives."

"Where is Siobhan?"

"She's in the garden. You will be pleased by the changes in her."

"And is she ready for…?"

"As long as you are gentle, yes."

He glanced down at his sleeping baby, a wave of love moving through him. "Can we go home now, or does he still need you?"

"Mior has begun solid food. I'm sure he'll be fine without my milk."

Dagda spied his wife sitting on a stone bench, her face turned toward the last rays of sun. Her hair was all afire, glinting gold and red. A fine gown of green silk hung demurely over her curves, her breasts and hips more substantial than they had been the last time he'd seen her. He lengthened his strides, his heart filled with love as her hurried toward her.

When she turned and saw him, her eyes lit up. A second later he enfolded into his arms. "You look so much better," he murmured, his face in her hair.

"And I feel it too. I've missed you, Dag. Have you seen our son? He has grown so, and he now…"

"Yes, I saw him with Frigg. She told me we could go home."

She pulled away. "Frigg met you?"

"She was in your room, Siobhan. She was feeding him when I got there."

She eyed him before taking his hand. "I can be a wife to you now," she murmured, tugging him back toward the castle.

Guilt made him silent as they made their way inside. She was too psychic for her own good. Had she always been like this?

When they reached the bedroom Frigg was still there, the baby ready to go and Siobhan's things packed into a small bag. Her gaze met his briefly before she turned her attention to Siobhan. "It will be several more months before you are fully back to yourself," she warned. "Do not overdo," she added with a sharp look at Dagda.

"Thank you," Siobhan said, moving to give the goddess a hug.

Dagda watched the two of them, noting the contrast in size, body type, and hair color. At this moment he desired both of them, a fantasy of the three of them in bed together entering his mind. He shifted from one foot to the other, anxious to be on his way.

"Before we go, I want you to tell me all about Katel," Siobhan announced.

Dagda stilled. "Can't it wait until we get home?"

Siobhan narrowed her eyes. "No more excuses, Dag."

Dagda glanced at Frigg who was watching him curiously. "I…I need to be in our own house with a drink in my hand before I can embark on all that."

Frigg smiled. "Yes. That sounds a good plan."

"See? Frigg agrees," he pleaded, his gaze on his wife.

Siobhan's lips thinned. "All right, but I will not be put off any longer. I expect to hear the truth tonight."

"It will be the wee hours by the time we reach home, Siobhan. Let's plan it for tomorrow evening, once I'm back from work."

She nodded and lifted the baby out of his basket, wrapping him into a heavy wool scarf she'd tied around her shoulder for the trip. Dagda frowned as he reached for her bag. He hadn't planned to go to work the next day, intending to spend it in bed with his wife, but with this looming over his head he had to come up with a strategy.

At the entrance Frigg pulled him aside, waiting until Siobhan was out of earshot. "You'd best be careful with your lies with this one. She's very intuitive."

He nodded, pressing her close for an instant before heading outside. Intuitive was putting it mildly. And if she learned of this latest betrayal, it would put her over the edge.

"You and Frigg seem to have bonded," Siobhan remarked as they prepared to go.

His breath caught as he picked her up in his arms. "I've known her for a very long time."

17

K at woke in her bed with her head splitting, the headache making it hard to even open her eyes. Something terrible had happened, she knew it, but she couldn't place it. A vague vision of a dark room, a dog being shot, and her father looming over her, swirled in her mind, confusing her even further. When she rose from bed she realized she was fully dressed, down to the tennis shoes on her feet. A moment later she was running for the bathroom to be sick.

It took a while for her head to stop spinning, her stomach contracting in pain after the violent vomiting. She knew she'd been drugged—it was the reason for her headache and the nausea. When she was finally able to rise from the tile floor, she turned on the shower and peeled off her filthy clothes, wondering how they got so covered in dirt. She showered quickly, a feeling of urgency moving through her—she was supposed to be somewhere…she was late.

As she fumbled around in her closet for something to wear, she asked herself what her last memory was. Had she been a victim of date rape? She saw herself walking home from Gwen's shop, the dog at her side. Pooka!

Images burst forth like fireworks, her mind ablaze with the shooting, the dust Pooka turned into. She was suddenly overcome with a black rage, tears flowing down her cheeks. When she waved her hands in the air sparks burst from her fingertips, landing on the floor to start tiny fires. As she hurried to put them out she remembered everything—being shut up in the cellar room, her father telling her he had to take her memories, her fury and accusing him of being afraid of her…asking about her mother; it all flooded back. She finished dressing and grabbed her keys and rushed out the door. He would pay for this…that bastard would pay for this!

Outside more sparks flew, people staring at her and giving her a wide berth. *Control,* she whispered to herself. *I have to control my anger,* but before she reached the shop, she'd started a fire in a dumpster and knocked a man down just by glaring at him. She hadn't meant to do it, it was only that her angry gaze had happened to land on him. When she went to help, he crab-walked away from her before rising to his feet and sprinting in the opposite direction.

She burst into the shop, surprising Gwen who stood talking with Airmid, both of them turning as a gust of wind blew papers off the desk. Gwen hurried toward her, picking up papers as she went. "Kat! Where have you been? I've been so worried!"

"He did it again!" Kat shouted. "He had me kidnapped and kept me in a cellar, and then he took my memories—except he didn't manage it this time," she ended triumphantly.

As she spoke, sparks flew around the room. Airmid waved a hand to put them out. "You need to calm yourself," she warned.

"I'm so angry!"

When the earth goddess touched her shoulder Kat immediately relaxed, her pulse slowing. She let out a long sigh, her taut shoulders dropping. "I asked him about Mom, but he didn't answer. I was in his office."

"Do you know where it is?"

She shook her head. "There was a cityscape filled with brick buildings and the weather was terrible."

"That could be many places," Airmid murmured, glancing at Gwen.

"I can find him," Kat muttered.

"You can? How?"

She glanced at Airmid. "I just know I can. It's why he's scared of me."

Airmid and Gwen exchanged a glance. "I suggest you learn to control yourself before you embark on *that* particular mission," Gwen said.

The next few weeks flew by as Airmid coached Kat on control, helping her recognize her moods before they came up and several calming breathing techniques. Most mornings Airmid went to Kat's apartment, leaving Gwen to run the shop. The goddess taught her a version of martial arts, slow moving hand movements combined with breath.

"I want to see Mom," Kat said one morning as they embarked on their usual exercises. She'd pushed the furniture back in her small living room so they'd have space to move around.

Airmid stopped the warm up exercises, focusing on Kat. "I'm sure you do, but she won't be the mom you remember."

"How do you know? Dad liked her the way she was—why would he change anything?"

"I doubt he had much control after bringing her back—she's bound to have differences, Kat."

"She has a baby."

"A baby? He told you that?"

Kat nodded. "He said he made her younger, but that doesn't mean she'll be different than how she was when I was a kid."

Airmid's eyes narrowed, her gaze moving to the open window. "This news changes things," she muttered.

"How so?"

"He's brought another illegitimate child into the world and with a woman who is supposed to be dead—his punishment will be even more severe."

"So, I'm illegitimate?"

"Your father is a god who had no business being with your mom. The audacity of doing this again is unforgivable."

"Not to mention the 'bringing her back from the dead' part."

"Exactly. I will have to report this. The sooner you find him the better. He *has* to face the consequences of his actions."

"You mean in Otherworld."

Her eyes darkened. "I mean Otherworld and Earth, Kat. I feel it every day, the malevolent energy that creeps across this world as well as in the realm of the gods."

Kat's thoughts turned dark, anger flooding her, but instead of acting on her emotions she took in a deep breath. And then another. "Is there any other way to stop it?"

Airmid shook her head, her eyes downcast. "I know it must seem odd, but it only takes one god's illegal behavior to put us at risk. The web has been torn, and it will unravel. How soon, no one knows, but we've both seen the results."

Kat thought of the gray trees, the feeling of desolation and the lack of life. "If Bran was here, he…"

Airmid looked up. "But Bran isn't here."

"Where is he?"

"I don't know, Kat. I've never seen him like he was that day."

Kat stilled, noticing Airmid's welling eyes, her lips pressed together. "You don't think he's coming back."

Airmid wiped a hand over her eyes. "I have to hope he will."

"He loves me, I know he does…"

"I'm sure he *did*."

Kat noticed the past tense and the look on her face. Bran had left in order to put her out of his mind—to stop loving her. And if he succeeded, she might never see him again.

18

Bran put one foot in front of the other, the heaviness he'd worn since he left Kat still with him. He'd traveled from Asgard, home of the Norse gods, to the desolate realm of Niflheim, the freezing land of mists and fog. It seemed fitting somehow to go where the biting wind took his breath, his feet frozen through his boots, and where the dragon, Nidhogg, ate the corpses of those who tried to survive here. Hel, the giantess, also inhabited this realm, ruling over the dead. Hel was the only daughter of Loki and the giantess, Angrboda. She had two brothers, the wolf, Fenrir, and a serpent, Jormundgandr.

Bran had yet to see the dragon or Hel, but he was acutely aware of the pain in his chest, the ice crystals coating his eyelashes and the fact that he had no heavy coat. As far as he could tell, nothing lived here besides Hel and the dragon, the waves of ice rippling toward him, impossible to travel across and everchanging. Yggdrasil was the tree of life that held all nine worlds within its limbs, and this realm was where the well of Hvergelmir had its origins, and where Yggdrasil's roots acquired its water. Hvergelmir was the origin of life and where it would all return. But at this moment Bran didn't care about that—his need to find shelter first and foremost in his mind.

Thoughts of death descended into the center of his being, his heart slowing as he grew colder. He couldn't feel his fingers, or his toes, his frown frozen in place. Even as a god he couldn't combat this kind of weather. He would succumb if he didn't find a place of shelter soon. The energy was wrong here, whether coming from him or the changes to the place, he wasn't sure. It didn't matter— nothing mattered anymore.

In Asgard he'd spoken with Odin regarding what Dagda had done and was continuing to do, but Odin had no interest in what he said, telling him that the Norse gods did not want to be involved in Otherworld's petty affairs. "Otherworld is miniscule compared to our nine worlds," he'd said disdainfully, sending Bran on his way. But Bran had seen the worried expression in the god's one eye; Odin had been lying when he intimated that he didn't care.

All worlds would soon be affected by Dagda's betrayal. Odin knew it as did all the gods in all the realms. The shift had already begun. Even here in Niflheim.

Time had gone by, how much he couldn't determine. He figured he'd be dead soon, which sounded good. He was a god, and normally gods did not go like this, alone and dying of exposure, but it seemed he'd bypassed all that, his wretchedness lessening his ability to keep his body from succumbing. Or maybe it was simply that he didn't care anymore. Kat's face drifted in and out of his mind where he huddled under an ice floe, he felt her body close to him, her soft lips on his. He let out a howl, the sound taken on the wind and sent spinning across the ice. His tears were frozen to his face, leaving a sheen of ice that felt like a mask. Instead of reconnecting to his power, he'd yielded to his emptiness. He was as hollow as a reed.

He was barely conscious when he felt his body lifted; his eyes were frozen shut, his limbs slack. He couldn't move, he couldn't speak, had no idea what it was that took him from what surely would have been his grave. The wind buffeted against him, cold and unrelenting, time seeming to flow like water. He was slipping further and further away as they traveled, awareness drifting on a sea of ice as his blood froze. He was unaware of anything for a long time, until his body fell, tumbling over and over to land so hard that he was sure some bones were broken. Everything went dark after that.

He woke slowly, realizing that his eyes were no longer frozen shut. Dark walls of stone surrounded him, tall and unclimbable. Above him he could see a tiny patch of gray where a hole gave way to the sky. When he finally pulled his gaze back to where he lay, he noticed the scattered whitened bones of others who had landed here. Sitting up took all his energy, his groan loud in his ears. A hiss and the movement of something big alerted him to the fact that he was not alone. A second later he was staring into the narrowed yellow-green eyes of a dragon, the exhaled breath fiery and red-yellow. For a moment he basked in the warmth until he realized the danger. He was in a pit with a dragon who had obviously devoured many others.

He scrambled to his feet and skittered away, his back

hitting the wall. The dragon was enormous, filling the space with his scaled body, his tapered claws scraping the dirt as he stared at Bran. "How did I get here?" Bran muttered, looking around for a hole he could crawl into.

"Hel brought you," the dragon replied.

Bran's mouth fell open in surprise. "You…you speak?"

"I have the knowledge of every language."

"Will you eat me?"

The dragon made a rumbling sound deep in his throat. "I eat the dead, not the living."

Bran breathed out a sigh of relief. "Hel thought I was dead."

"That is correct."

He glanced up at the hole so very far away. "How do I get out of here?"

"When Hel returns with another corpse, perhaps she will assist you. Otherwise you are stuck here."

"And I will die of starvation."

The dragon made a motion with its head, signaling yes. "But you will be warm when you go," he said, making the rumbling sound again.

"A dragon with a sense of humor," Bran muttered. As night came on and the temperature dropped, he pulled on a heavy winter coat he found in the pit. It smelled of death but at least it was warm.

It was two days and nights later before Bran began to seriously worry. If it hadn't been for the stream trickling in the back of the pit he would already have died of thirst.

"What if Hel doesn't come back?" he asked the dragon the morning of the third day.

"I have nothing to say on that subject," Nidhogg replied. "As I recall you wanted to die—has something changed? If you die your body will feed me—at least that should make you happy."

"Why would that make me happy? And as to my former wish to die, it's gone now, partly due to our conversations."

The rumbling sound of mirth made the dragon's body shake. "You are a strange one, Bran ap Llyr. If you make it out of here alive, will you seek out this woman you have talked about ad nauseum?"

Bran was the one to laugh this time. "I hope so, although if her father, Dagda, catches me, I'm sure he or one of his minions will kill me."

"Dagda. I know this name, although I cannot recall why."

"He's from Otherworld and the same rank as Odin; I'm sure they've had dealings over the centuries."

"Possibly. It is Odin who is responsible for my being here in this prison."

"Why haven't you simply flown out?"

Nidhogg glanced upward toward the square of grayish light. "Have you noticed my size? I cannot fit through that tiny hole. This is my prison until that opening breaks apart or I die."

"But how did you get in here in the first place?"

A wistful look came into his slanted yellowish eyes. "I was smaller back then. He clipped my wings so I was forced to remain on the ground."

Bran pressed his back into the stone wall, trying to

ignore his aching and hollow stomach. "What did you do to anger Odin?"

A puff of flame came out of his mouth as he spoke. "I argued with him over his decision to leave Hel here in Niflheim. It was done only because the other gods could not stand to look upon her."

"I haven't seen her so I can't speak to that."

The dragon drew himself up, blue flame racing toward where Bran sat.

"Why did you do that?" Bran asked, huddling back in the shadows.

"You are as bad as the rest of them if you think that being hideous is a reason to be left alone in the coldest and most desolate realm in all nine worlds!"

"I didn't say that!" Bran cried out, putting more distance between himself and the dragon. "But if all the gods were in agreement, then…"

"Then, what? Hel is Loki's daughter. Fenrir, Loki's wolf son, isn't too beautiful either, but you do not see him here. Being labeled the queen of the dead is not enough reward for a life spent utterly alone."

Bran decided to stay silent after that, afraid of angering the dragon. He knew Nidhogg was hungry. The idea of dying slowly while his skin was burned off, and then being eaten, was not at all appealing.

The patch of gray sky had turned to mauve when Bran heard a heavy sound from above, a contorted and stinking naked body hurtling past where he sat. The dragon roused himself, sniffing the air before moving to the corpse. "Call to her, Nidhogg," Bran hissed. "I need food!"

"We just got food," the dragon replied, his jaws closing over a grayish leg.

The bone cracked apart as the dragon chewed, the stench of the decayed flesh making Bran gag. "I can't eat that. Please call to her."

"You call to her," Nidhogg answered. "I am busy."

Bran cupped his hands around his mouth and shouted as loud as he could, but the sound of his voice seemed to ricochet off the rocks and went nowhere. "Please!" he begged.

The dragon glanced up, an arm with a stiff hand attached sticking out of his jaws. "Hel!" he bellowed, before resuming his feast.

"What is it, Dragon?" a voice called back. "Is this corpse not to your liking?"

"It is a bit old, but that is not why I called to you. It seems this body you brought me a few days ago was still alive. And now he wants to leave."

An enormous face appeared in the square of rosy light, turning the pit dark. "And who is it that wishes to leave?"

"It is I, Bran ap Llyr, god of prophecy and ravens," Bran shouted. "I will die if I don't get food."

Hel didn't reply for a minute or two, her face withdrawing. Minutes passed before a rope appeared, waving like a snake as it was lowered. Bran grabbed hold of it and tied it around his waist. "If there is a way to release you, I will find it," he told the dragon as Hel began to tug him upward.

Nidhogg stopped chewing, his strange yellow serpent eyes trained on Bran. "I thank you for that," he said.

As Bran rose closer to the top he had to close his eyes against the brightness. Being in a pit for a week had made him light sensitive, despite the gray pall that lay across the vista as night approached. When he opened them again he saw a giant woman bending over him, one side of her face turned toward him as she helped undo the rope. She wasn't beautiful, but the eye he could see was dark and intelligent, her skin smooth. *She isn't ugly*, he thought to himself. It was only when she turned that he saw the skeleton that comprised the other side of her body. No skin covered her, sinews and muscles straining as she lifted him to his feet. He recoiled, rebelling against the sight of her, his insides heaving.

"So, human. What will you do now?" she asked.

"I'm not human," he answered, keeping his eyes averted. "I'm Bran ap Llyr, god of ravens, prophecy, and protection."

She let out a bellow. "Human, god, it makes no difference to me. I am a queen, and I suppose, a goddess, although as you can see, I've been placed where no one will ever behold my grotesque visage."

Bran heard the wretchedness in her tone, sympathy lessening his horror. He steeled himself, looking upon her fully. She was a giant, casting a shadow where she loomed over him, her good side filled out in the natural curves of a woman, the other side like some dead and rotted thing flung up on a desolate shore in the middle of nowhere. "How did you get this way?"

"I was born this way."

"And nothing Loki could do to help you?"

She shook her head, the lank straggly hair on one side of her head sending ice crystals flying around her. "I am as I am meant to be."

When Bran took in a breath, the tiny hairs in his nose

froze. A gust of wind blew the hood of his coat back, his eyes watering before his tears turned instantly to ice. "Odin's ghost, it's cold."

Hel rumbled with laughter. "Odin's ghost? I wish."

"Sorry—it's a saying we have in Otherworld."

"Do you need transport or will you try and find your way out of here on your own?"

"I have a lot of things to think about, so I'll go on my way alone. But how can I find something I can eat?"

"I will take you to the pool where the salmon swim. It is a bit warmer there. If you are who you say you are, you will have no problem catching one and cooking it."

"Because I'm a god?"

"Do you not have powers?"

"Well, yes, but I haven't tested them in a while."

"That was obvious by the state you were in when I found you."

Bran stared up at her. "You knew I wasn't dead?"

"Yes. It is why I threw you into the pit with Nidhogg. I decided that if you died he would have a meal, and if you lived, the warmth would sustain you." She held out her good hand and he grabbed it.

The pool sat in a cleft between two black stone hills. A sheen of ice layered the surfaces of the rocks, but there was no ice on the dark water. "It is fed by an underground spring," Hel explained. "It comes from the same source as the well that feeds Yggdrasil's roots."

Bran had a sense of protection here, something instantly calming inside of him. He also knew that the salmon represented wisdom and inner truth. "It's peaceful here."

"Yes. You may or may not be blessed with the salmon's appearance. If it comes to you, it does so to teach through its flesh. Once you eat it you will understand where you've been and where you are going. Change is in your future."

"And it's okay to eat it?"

Hel nodded, one side of her mouth turning up in a smile. "It will give you what you need, both physically and spiritually."

"And if it doesn't come?" Bran rubbed his empty belly.

"If it doesn't come then you are on the wrong path and will need to find another way."

"And die from hunger."

"If you are truly a god, you will not die."

Once Hel left, Bran sat by the pool, staring into the opaque water. His mouth watered with the idea of cooked fish; he'd already gathered the wood he would need to start the fire, and whittled the stick to use for a spit. His knife lay next to him, ready to spear the fish once it appeared. But so far he hadn't seen anything but his own reflection, a sight that shocked him. He'd lost weight, his cheeks sunken, and the hair hanging around his face was lank and dirty. His eyes had lost their luster, a permanent mark etched into the skin between his brows. He looked human and old, not at all like a god. Had he lost who he was? When Kat's face loomed up in his mind, he waved it away. They were no longer destined to be together. He'd given up on that a long time ago. Somehow spilling his guts to the dragon had cleansed him of her.

But when his tired eyes closed, she was there. When he woke again it was out of a dream in which they were making love, their connection like a holy thing; a precious jewel of boundless worth. His frozen fingers moved to the pendant hanging around his neck, the metal so cold his fingers stuck to it.

19

"Sir, may I speak to you for a moment?"

Dagda raised his head from the pile of papers on his desk. Things were thoroughly out of control, both here and abroad. "What is it, Jones?"

"I've been doing as you asked, tailing Katel to see what she's up to, but there's something strange going on with her. The other day I'm sure I saw sparks coming out of the ends of her fingers."

"What?" Dagda jumped to his feet. "Are you sure?"

"Yes, sir, I am."

Dagda narrowed his eyes at Jones, wondering how much the guy had figured out. Telling him what was going on was out of the question. "What do you think is going on?"

"Well...I've never believed in the supernatural, but when I shot her dog, the thing disappeared in a cloud of dust, and the other day she started a couple of fires from sparks from her fingers. Is she some sort of a witch?"

"Don't be moronic. There is no such thing as a real witch. Whatever she's playing at is only that...some sort of parlor trick. Now please do as I asked and keep a watch on her. I want to know her every move."

After Jones left Dagda paced his office. He felt like his life was closing on him. His daughter was no longer responding to his attempts to stop her powers, his wife was asking questions and demanding answers, and his business dealings were out of control. He let out a roar of anger and pounded his fist on the mahogany desk, cracking the wood. He'd put Siobhan off for a week now, telling her lie after lie about why now wasn't a good time to talk. Tonight he would have to come up with something or there would be hell to pay. What in hell would he tell her? One scenario after another passed through his mind, each one discarded as he realized the flaws she would surely detect. What if he just told her the bloody fucking truth? Their daughter was an all too powerful goddess, who if not kept in check would ruin their fucking lives? And if he couldn't stop her, Kat would take away everything he'd worked so hard to build, including his life on earth with Siobhan. He could not let that happen, especially now that he had a son.

When he came through the door that afternoon Siobhan was there to greet him. He pulled her into his arms and kissed her, feeling her softness and smelling her vanilla and citrus scent. He wanted her very badly. But when he tugged her toward the stairs, she stopped him. "Remember what you promised."

"I need you, Siobhan. I promise to tell you after…can you trust me on that?"

"I've been waiting for over a week now, Dag."

"I know, but I'm…I had a shit day and I need to…"

Siobhan smiled. "I know how it calms you. But if you put me off after you've had your way with me, I will…"

He laughed and lifted her into his arms, hurrying up the stairs to their bedroom.

He undressed her and placed her on the bed, barely able to get his clothes off fast enough. Gods she was beautiful. She'd filled out since her ordeal, her body rounded and rosy, her breasts firm. "Is the baby asleep?" he asked, looking around for Mior's basket.

"You asked me to move him into the spare room, so that's where he is. But I warn you, if he needs me…"

Dagda barely heard her, his focus on her lips, her breasts and the secret place between her legs. When she let out a low moan, he knew she was there with him, his heat and hers mingling as he pressed inside her.

It was dark outside when he'd finally had his fill. Siobhan was asleep, her tangled hair spread across the pillow, her breath deep. He kissed her lightly and rose from the rumpled bed and headed into the bathroom to shower.

When he came out Siobhan was sitting up, the baby at her breast. "He still likes this best," she said.

He laughed. "Who wouldn't?"

"I haven't begun dinner. Can you run down and turn the oven on?"

"What temperature?"

"400* please. I have a tray of cut-up vegetables to be roasted and your favorite cut of beef waiting to be barbequed."

"Wine?" he asked, pulling on a pair of sweatpants.

She nodded. "Once Mior's fed I'll join you downstairs.

I plan to hold you to your promise, so be prepared."

Dagda nodded, a frisson of nerves moving through him as he reran his latest lie through his mind.

He was well into his second glass of whiskey when Siobhan appeared wearing a slinky dressing gown. "Are you trying to drive me insane?" he asked, pouring wine into a glass and holding it out.

She laughed. "You make me feel sexy, Dag."

"You are sexy."

"I usually feel like a frumpy housewife with a cranky baby. I barely have time to shower. Hardly what I'd call sexy."

He shook his head, tugging her down next to him on the couch. "Not what I see," he murmured, kissing her neck.

She pulled away and stared at him. "It's time to fess up, Dag. Where is our daughter?"

Dagda took a hefty gulp of whiskey and placed the glass on the coffee table. "She's dangerous to us, Siobhan. I've been trying to keep her powers at bay, but I may not be able to manage it anymore. She will rat us out and it will be the end of what we have here."

Siobhan's mouth dropped open, her hazel eyes going wide. "What makes you think she would do this? Have you asked her? She's our daughter and I want to see her—not just see her, but be with her, and talk to her. If you know where she is, and how to reach her, I expect you to make this happen." She slammed her glass down and rose from the couch, heading into the kitchen to deal with dinner.

Dagda stared after her, noting the tension in her

shoulders and rigid back. When she got like this there was no reasoning with her. When Mior let out a piercing shriek he hurried upstairs. But even the sight of his son couldn't bring him out of the funk he'd sunk into. He lifted Mior out of his crib and carried him back downstairs, depositing the baby into his new bouncy chair.

Once Mior was settled Dagda headed outside to start the barbeque. He glanced around the enormous yard, thinking about what they'd created with the massive amounts of money he made. They had a full-time gardener, a yard filled with flowers and trees, a koi pond and an arbor covered with roses. The leaves had turned with the change in weather, their bright colors adding to the beauty. A veil passed in front of his eyes, the world going dark for a moment as he contemplated losing it all.

20

K at's life was now broken into periods of work, periods of training, and periods of rest. She fell into bed exhausted each night, her dreams merely repeats of what she'd been taught that day. Airmid had turned into her best friend, the one she talked with when she had misgivings or felt insecure or worried. She barely remembered the life they'd shared before, all her anger and upset about Airmid's reaction to Bran pretty much gone. Kat now understood the reasons for her behavior, her own knowledge of what it meant to be a goddess growing as the days and weeks flew by.

"Shall we make a trip to the forest today?" Airmid asked Kat on the morning of her fourth week of mentoring. "I think it's time to test you and see if there are other abilities that have yet to show themselves."

Kat smiled and held the door wide. "Shall we take along a thermos of your famous tea?"

Fall was now fully upon them, the days cold and windy, the nights sometimes dropping to freezing. *What happened to the summer?* Kat asked herself as she pulled on a heavy sweater. Time seemed to have sped up.

The forest was bleak, and the grayness had spread since Kat's last trip here. A colorless pall hung over the trees, dull smudges taking away the green of life. Many of the leaves had already fallen, grayed out on the ground like weathered photographs. The limbs were bare and lifeless, and the energy felt wrong—like a sudden drop in barometric pressure. Her senses picked up the odor of rot, the sound of whispering and rustling. She saw creatures in the understory, hairless and pale, their backs hunched with deformed spines that stuck out. She caught sight of black eyes, heard them hiss as they ran to hide. They mostly stayed out of sight, but what she'd seen of them creeped her out. "What are they?" she whispered.

Airmid's eyes narrowed. "The Dubh are beings who steal the light. It's why this forest has no color. They normally live deep underground, but Dagda has created a rift and they are now able to get through."

Kat moved along the trail, keeping on the look-out for the creatures as she went. "What do they want?" she murmured, trying to make as little noise as she could.

"They want our light. If this rift is not mended, they will take it all and leave us with a gray world and gray minds."

Kat stopped to face the earth goddess. "Gray minds?"

Airmid nodded. "We will have no joy, no contentment, no love. Our minds will be as colorless as the forest you see in front of you."

Kat shuddered, trying to imagine it. It didn't seem

possible, and yet…she knew it was. "What can we do?"

Airmid took hold of her arm, tugging her back the other way. "We must repair the fissure, and that requires finding Dagda and sending him back to Otherworld."

Kat knew she could track him and find him, but her initial anger after her imprisonment had dissipated; sending him back to Otherworld was no longer at the top of her priority list. For one thing he was with her mother, and she had a baby brother now. Her mother would be devastated, and the baby would be left without a father. With the knowledge she now had, it no longer seemed right to her—but if she didn't, the entire world might be stripped of everything good.

"What is it, Kat?" Airmid asked, peering at her.

"Nothing—just thinking."

"You had a terrible frown on your face. Is it what I just told you?"

"Partly. Is there any other way to get rid of the Dubh?"

There was a lengthy silence before Airmid said, "Not that I know of."

Was the entire weight of the world resting on Kat's shoulders? If so, she wasn't up to the task, she thought morosely, hurrying down the path.

Once they reached the apartment, Airmid left her there to change, heading off to Cerridwen's Cosmetic Cauldron. "Take your time, Kat. I have a few things I need to discuss with Gwen."

Kat closed the door behind her, wondering why Airmid didn't wait so that they could walk over together.

Kat was about to enter the cosmetic shop when she heard Airmid mention her name and Gwen's mumbled response. The window was closed, as was the door—her hearing had definitely improved. She stopped with her hand on the handle and listened.

"She didn't sense anything that I could tell. I fear she is not as strong as we imagined. I doubt seriously that she can combat what's happening."

"What about her training?"

Airmid let out a low humorless laugh. "She has control of her anger now. But shooting sparks out of your fingers is hardly what I'd call powers. We're dealing with supernatural entities that will require a lot more than that."

"Then why would Dagda be so set on keeping her from knowing who she is?"

"Maybe he assumed something that isn't true. He is an egotist, after all—he probably thinks that any child that came from his loins has to be the most powerful goddess in the universe."

Gwen chuckled, their voices fading as they moved into the back room.

Kat paused, trying to decide what to do. She *had* sensed things in the forest, she just hadn't mentioned it to Airmid. And as far as her anger, it seemed that whatever was manifesting arrived when it was needed. For some reason being off the hook for whatever the goddesses' thought was her destiny, didn't make her feel any lighter. Something was definitely brewing in the back of her mind, some plan her subconscious seemed to be hatching. Should she explain this to Airmid and Gwen, or let them go on thinking she didn't have what it took to be a goddess? She turned the handle and walked into the shop.

It was late afternoon when she left the shop to head home. The day had been fraught with tension, the overheard conversation making her feel uncomfortable and more than a little angry. Airmid and Gwen had acted like everything was normal, but Kat had seen the furtive looks that passed between them. Before she left for the day, Kat told Airmid that she needed a few days off from the training. "I have things to process," she said, trying to smile.

Airmid seemed surprised, but took it all in stride. "Will you be here tomorrow?"

Kat shook her head. "I need time alone."

"All right then," Airmid had said uncertainly, giving her a quick hug. "Let me know when you're ready to begin again."

Kat wondered why Airmid felt it necessary to 'begin again' if Kat had no goddess powers. She felt the anger rise and stopped it before it took her over, waving gaily as she left the shop.

The sky had gone from blue to nearly black in the past half hour, as though the weather itself was being changed by her dark mood. She laughed, wondering if any god or goddess could affect such things with their minds. But when the wind began to blow wildly, sending trash skittering down the street, she wondered. Calming her mind took some time, but as it finally settled, the wind settled with it. *Coincidence?* she asked herself.

21

The heavy knock brought Kat out of her meditation, adrenaline shooting through her veins. Whoever this was at her door was not someone she wanted to see. But instead of ignoring it, she rose to her feet and moved cautiously to peer through the peephole. What she saw on the other side stopped her breath. She threw the door open, glaring at Dagda hulking in the hallway. "What are *you* doing here?"

"Is that any way to greet your father?" he asked, shoving by her.

"I don't want you here."

Dagda gazed down on her, a smile curling at the corners of his wide mouth. "I only came because your mother forced me. She wants to see you, Katel."

"My mother sent you?"

"Yes, and she wouldn't take no for an answer." He gazed into the distance, a wistful expression on his face. "She is something, that mother of yours."

"And? What do *you* want from me?"

He frowned, bringing his focus back to hers. "I want

you to come with me. I promised I'd return with you."

Kat just stared at him for several moments before her wits came back to her. "I want to see her too, but...I thought I would come to you."

"And how exactly would you have done that?"

Kat grinned and shrugged.

"You little minx—are you saying you could find me?"

She nodded. "Just give me a moment to get my coat and put on my shoes."

When Kat returned a few minutes later Dagda was sprawled across her couch, his booted feet propped up on her coffee table. He'd taken off his long black coat revealing the fine linen shirt he wore underneath. His piercing blue eyes met hers. "Are you ready?" he asked, reaching for his wool coat.

"Where are we going exactly?"

"I thought you said you could find me."

"I *can* find you, but I don't know how I would do it. I just know I could. I'm pretty sure you don't live in this city."

"You're right about that. Hope you don't mind traveling through the ether."

"The ether? How would we..."

Dagda grabbed her by the hand and in the next moment she felt like the world and any gravity had dropped away. Colors whirled, wind rushing by her ears. It took only a few minutes before they had dropped into a neighborhood of enormous houses, each with probably four to five acres of land around them. He led her toward a wrought iron gate between two stone pillars, basalt ravens perched on top. He punched in numbers on a key pad and the gate swung open.

Ahead of her she saw the Georgian style brick mansion

covered in Virginia creeper that had turned russet, the gardens spreading away in a riot of fall color. Japanese maples had turned red and orange, many of the leaves already on the ground. An arbor caught her eye, the wisteria and rose vines twisting through it, nearly bare. A pond shone like molten silver in the distance, a haze of water falling from the mouth of a dragon sculpture in the middle. She drew her coat close as the wind came up, nerves making her shake. "It's beautiful," she said, turning to Dagda next to her.

"The best money can buy," he agreed.

"How long have you been here?"

"Only since I brought your mother back the second time. It's been nearly two years now."

Kat thought of her mother's death, the long hard road she'd had to travel to recover. She remembered Dagda's first attempt to resurrect her and the botched robotic person Siobhan had been. Would she be like that this time? The thought of seeing her filled kat with equal amounts of dread and excitement. "Will she remember me?"

"Of course she remembers you, Kat. It's why she sent me to get you."

"But you told me you'd made her young—how can she remember her life before?"

He let out a long sigh. "At first she didn't, but after the baby was born something happened to her, something I can't explain."

Kat glanced at his strong profile. "The baby...that's right, I have a brother."

"Indeed you do." When he strode ahead of her up the long driveway she hurried to catch up.

Before they reached the front door, it opened, a woman who looked to be in her early thirties standing there with a wide smile on her face. A second later she was pulled into familiar arms, the scent of lemon and vanilla she remembered from her childhood bombarding her senses. Tears welled and spilled over.

"Come in," Siobhan murmured, tugging her inside and closing the door.

"Mom," Kat murmured, overwhelmed with emotion. "I…I've missed you so much."

Siobhan smiled sadly. "And I you. Your father has taken his own sweet time in bringing you back to me, haven't you, Dagda?" she said, turning to the hulking presence next to them.

Kat was surprised by the cowed look on his face, his eyes shining with love. "But I did it, didn't I, my sweet?"

"Yes," she said, touching his arm. "Thank you."

When a high-pitched wail sounded, Siobhan hurried away. "Take Kat into the living room, would you Dag? I need to get the baby."

Kat watched her mother's familiar back as she headed up the steps, something inside her seeming to finally settle. Her mother was exactly as she remembered her.

Dagda touched her shoulder. "Follow me."

"You don't want me here, do you?" she asked as she followed him across the wide foyer and into another room.

He turned. "I was afraid of what you might do, Katel. I remember how against the resurrection you were before I…"

"Before you took my memories the first time?"

He nodded. "You were not in favor of what I planned to do."

"No, but I finally gave in. And then you screwed everything up."

He sighed and ran agitated fingers through his dark curls. "I admit the first time was a disaster. But this time…and then the birth…it's as though she…" At that moment Siobhan entered the room carrying a pudgy baby.

"Kat, meet your baby brother, Mior." She held him out.

Kat's heart melted as she took the baby in her arms. He smelled of talcum and lemon, his hands waving in the air. He looked up at her and made a gurgling sound as he focused on her face. "How old is he now?"

"He was born on the first of May—Beltane, which, according to your father, is very auspicious," she added, glancing at Dagda. "He's nearly six months old."

Kat placed the baby on the floor and sat next to him, transfixed by his canny look and how beautiful he was. "He's gorgeous," she gushed, touching his shiny black curls.

"Takes after your father," Siobhan said.

"He has your face shape," Kat said, tracing his chin with her finger. He grabbed her hand and pulled her forefinger into his mouth.

"He's teething," Siobhan explained, "and as far as his face shape, it's the same as yours."

Kat glanced up to see her father hovering over Siobhan like a mother hen, his hands on her shoulders. He bent to kiss her neck before he left the room, announcing that he was going to make tea.

"Your father is so good to us," Siobhan whispered, sitting on the floor next to Kat.

"He certainly loves you," Kat murmured, her gaze on the baby.

"He loves you too, Kat."

Kat turned her gaze to her mother. "Did you know he had me kidnapped and locked in a basement for an entire week? He took my memories, Mom. Luckily I've got some goddess in me and it didn't work."

Siobhan's eyes widened in alarm. "He wouldn't do that—he couldn't."

"He's afraid I'll rat him out. You do know that he's wanted back in Otherworld to stand trial. Being here is illegal for him."

"I did know that," she murmured, "but it's hard for me to believe that he'd…"

"What are you two talking about?" Dagda asked, placing a tray with three cups, a teapot and a sugar and creamer on the coffee table next to where they sat on the floor.

"Kat just told me what you did to her, Dag. How could you?"

Dagda's face crumpled. "I…I was afraid she'd…"

"She'd what? She's your daughter!"

Dagda glared at Kat. "You shouldn't have mentioned this," he growled. "She's not strong enough."

"Don't speak to her like that!" Siobhan cried out. "Explain to me why you did what you did."

Dagda sat down on the couch and put his head in his hands. "Kat is a goddess, Siobhan. She has powers and I couldn't risk having her use them on me."

"Why would she?"

"Because she was against me bringing you back to life. I just couldn't risk it."

"I wasn't against it, but the first time, when…"

"What first time?" Siobhan asked sharply.

"He botched it," Kat told her. "You were like a robot."

Siobhan paled. "Like a…but I thought that…I thought…" She gasped and a second later she'd fainted, her body crumpling to the floor.

"What have you done?" Dagda roared, rushing toward Siobhan. His arms went around her and he picked her up. "Watch Mior."

Kat heard his feet pounding up the stairs, the bang of a door being opened too forcefully. When the baby looked up at her she pulled him into her lap. "I'm sorry," she murmured, tears falling. "Why did I tell her all that?" She buried her face in his soft curls.

She was in the garden with the baby in her arms when she heard Dagda's voice behind her. "First you try to kill my wife and now you're kidnapping my baby?"

She whirled around. "Your wife is my mother! Why would I want to harm her?"

His dark gaze bored into her. "Why would you bring all that up?"

"I thought she knew—why didn't you tell her?"

"It was a terrible time. I wanted to spare her all that."

"Is she okay?"

Dagda grabbed the baby out of her arms. "She is now, no thanks to you."

"I'm sorry. I didn't mean to…"

"That's your problem—you never mean to do the things you do, but…"

Kat glared at him. "What else have I done?"

Dagda held the baby up in the air, making him chortle. "I've felt your anger, Kat. I know what you're capable of.

If it was turned on your mother it could kill her."

"I would never harm her and you know it. I have no idea what I'm capable of."

"You're my daughter, which should tell you something. Why do you think I took your memories? Telling your mother about all that was unkind."

"So, she doesn't know about the cruel side of you? It isn't my fault that you've been lying to her." A wind suddenly came up, clouds right above them turning nearly black, a vortex churning like the beginnings of a funnel cloud.

Dagda gazed upward, a frown marring his forehead. "Are you doing that?"

"I don't know—am I?"

"You're angry."

"So? Does that mean I can start a storm?"

Dagda grabbed her arm and dragged her back to the house. "Yes, it does," he muttered, shoving her inside.

Kat had calmed and was examining the antique furniture, the lush Persian rugs and the ancient tapestries on the walls when Siobhan appeared, her face ashen. "I'm sorry for that," she said, joining Kat on the couch.

"It's my fault," Kat said. "I didn't know he hadn't told you." She turned to glare at her father sitting in a chair, Mior asleep in his arms.

"I...sometimes it's hard for me to take in information— it's as though I go into overload. Your father explained why he did what he did to you, but I still can't condone it. In his defense it happened right after Mior was born, when I lay between life and death."

"I didn't know about that."

"The birth was difficult and your father had to take me to Odin's castle to seek help from his wife, Frigg."

Kat glanced over at Dagda who was staring raptly at his son. "Why didn't you tell me any of this?"

Dagda raised his head. "When would I have had the chance? It's not like we visit on a regular basis."

"That day in your office, for instance. That would have been a good time to share."

Dagda shook his head. "I was attempting to keep you under control, Katel. Why would I open up about your mother?"

"It would have made me more sympathetic. As it was, I was furious with you."

"And discovered a new ability as a result."

Kat frowned. "How'd you know?"

"Jones came back with a story about sparks flying out of your fingertips as well as the disappearing act you pulled when he tried to shoot the dog." He chuckled. "I told him he'd imagined it."

"Yes, well…why did he kill Pooka?"

"Because a puka is a protection spirit. She was keeping me from finding you."

"Sweetheart, why don't we talk of more pleasant things?" Siobhan asked.

Kat let out a long sigh. "I cannot tell you how wonderful it is to see you again, Mom. I…"

"I know, dear. It is for me too. Now tell me about your life aside from this cat and mouse game you've been playing with your father. Do you have a man in your life?"

Kat glanced at her father who was watching her with a

frown. Mentioning Bran right now would start it up all over again—she blamed Dagda for his disappearance. She felt caught between her love of her mom and her complicated relationship with her father. There wasn't a subject she could imagine bringing up that wouldn't cause some sort of a rift. "As much as I love being with you, Mom, I should be getting back," she said, gazing at her apologetically.

Dagda rose and carried the baby over to Siobhan. "Isn't it nearly time to feed him?"

Siobhan gathered him close. "When he wakes I'll feed him. Now Kat, when will you visit again?"

Kat glanced at Dagda. "It's up to Dag," she answered.

"Since when do you call him Dag?"

Kat sighed. "Since he stopped acting like my father."

The trip back was the same as the trip there, Kat slightly dizzy by the time Dagda deposited her outside her apartment. "So, what happens now?" she asked him as she searched in her pocket for her key.

"If you keep me apprised of any new abilities, I will let you be, but as soon as I hear of any treachery, I will be very unhappy. Do you understand?"

"If you're trying to scare me it isn't working. Mom and I have reconnected now, and she's on my side. She would never let you hurt me."

"Who said anything about hurting? There are other ways to make your life miserable, Katel."

"And I'm your one and only daughter. What a bastard you are."

Dagda let out a roar of laughter. "You take after me."

"I do not!" She stuck the key in the lock and turned it,

not even looking at him as she pushed the door open and slammed it in his face. She threw the deadbolt across, not that that would do any good against a god, but the heavy clunk of it made her feel better. She could hear him chuckling on the other side, the sound of it making her blood boil.

22

Bran was dozing when the fish appeared, his eyes opening just in time to see it swimming away. He picked up his knife and lunged for it, tumbling into the freezing water as his knife made purchase. "I'm sorry," he murmured, watching it flail. As he took hold of it and climbed out of the pool, the salmon's dark pupil met his, its body going still. Something was transmitted in that moment, an understanding passing between them about the circle of life and what it meant. The salmon died to feed him, his own mortality up to the whims of the gods. There was a cycle for everything and a purpose that went along with it. With the world out of balance that purpose was distorted and lost.

He lit his fire using a trick he'd learned as a boy that had to do with rubbing the steel knife against the dark stone, and ripping a bit of his sleeve off to catch the sparks. Once the fire was going, he pushed the whittled stick through the salmon's body and held it over the flame until it turned a golden color. A second later he pulled off chunks of meat, burning his fingers as he stuffed them in his mouth. As he chewed the pink flesh, he had visions of other times and realms, his involvement in some faraway war taking over his senses. He was still a god, dressed in robes, but instead of presiding over a sumptuous banquet hall or meeting, he held a sword and a warrior woman stood by his side. Her hair was brown gold, her familiar face and shape dear to him. When he turned to her and met her gaze his heart turned over with love. She was his mate, his woman, and the mother of his children.

A roaring came to his ears as the enemy approached, one hundred strong, their steeds as black as night. When they crested the hill it was only he and his woman who stood to face them. *How could it be?* he thought, *Just the two of us against all of them?* It wasn't possible that they would live through this.

When the fish was gone Bran lay down next to the pool. His belly was full but his heart had been split in two.

Bran wasn't sure how long he lay there. At some point he woke and climbed the slippery basalt to the top of the hill, glad to feel the blast of icy air on his face. He braced against it and pulled his coat closed around his body as he made his way along the narrow path. He had no idea where he was going, only that he knew he should be going somewhere. The message he'd received didn't make much sense to him—the war, the woman he knew and loved, the impossibility of remaining alive. It seemed steeped in the past, but was it a metaphor for his future?

There were dreams too, dreams of other realms so desolate that he could barely stand to look upon them. A feeling that all was lost. As he walked, he let his mind play over it, hoping for some insight, but instead of insight he felt emptied out and dead to himself, as though his life had no meaning. "Why didn't you help me?" he shouted. "You were supposed to show me the way!"

Bran yearned for the green of Otherworld, the gods and goddesses who were like brothers and sisters to him, but he knew that Dagda's treachery had changed it all. He had nowhere to go, nowhere to be, his misery so profound that he wanted to lie down and freeze to death. But something drove him on, some tiny part of him that still dared to dream. What did the visions mean? How could he interpret the impossible war and Kat standing next to him amidst insurmountable odds? Was he part of her future? Was it up to the two of them to save the world?

After he'd screamed and yelled to gods that would never hear him, it was as though a cleansing wind blew through. He had no more thoughts of any kind, his only awareness the biting cold seeping through his boots and the wind whistling around his ears. When he caught sight of the wave of snow and ice coming toward him, he thought he was imagining it, watching it for several moments before a blast of ice blinded him. He was instantly awake and utterly alive, his instinct for survival kicking in as he turned and ran. But the roaring avalanche kept coming, the waves devouring him as the mass of snow and ice surged over him and kept going.

23

"**K**at, are you there?" Airmid called.

Kat stared at her bolted door, her head pounding from the wine she'd drunk the night before. "Go away and leave me alone."

"What is it? Did I do something? Please let me in."

"I need to be alone, Airmid. I have some thinking to do."

"Haven't you done enough of that? I dropped by yesterday and you weren't here—either that or you decided not to answer the door. Gwen and I are worried about you."

"Why? According to you I have no goddess powers—I obviously don't need your help."

There was a long silence in which Kat heard Airmid's sharp intake of breath. She could almost see her mind trying to come up with the right thing to say. "You overheard our conversation the other day," she finally offered.

"Yes, I did. You have no idea what's going on with me. Right now I'd like to pursue my own training without your opinions about what I can or can't accomplish."

"You need my input, Kat. If you've been keeping things from me, I need to know so that I can guide you."

"I don't need your guidance!" Kat shouted. "Now go away!" When Kat waved her hand, she heard a thump on the other side of the door, followed by a hiss of surprise.

"That's what I'm talking about," Airmid muttered. "You haven't been sharing."

Kat knew Airmid could come inside if she wanted to. No locks would keep her out. Right now, she was respecting Kat's wishes, but…Kat visualized a barrier, a membrane of protection, hoping that just thinking about it would make it be. She didn't know if had worked or not when she heard Airmid's boots thumping down the stairs.

Kat glanced around her dingy apartment, the clothes she'd left strewn across the tiny living room, the unwashed dishes in her sink. She wanted something better for herself, a new life, a new beginning. Working at Gwen's shop was getting her nowhere; Airmid and Gwen had already decided her fate. Would she ever see Bran again? Where was he? Maybe if she called to him through the ether he'd hear her—but what were the odds of that happening? And yet so many things she hadn't thought possible had already happened, like the storm that Dagda had attributed to her anger. Maybe it was time to be open to all possibilities. She picked up the clothes, depositing them into her clothes hamper, and then filled the sink with warm soapy water. Best to start with what was right in front of her.

Washing dishes and cleaning up left her mind free to wander, possible scenarios rising up in her mind. Oddly, she wanted to talk to her father. If anyone knew what she was capable of, it was he. But how to reach him? He'd always found her, not the other way around…and yet she'd told him she could track him down. Maybe it was time to test those theories. She thought back to the feeling she had when that idea had first gone through her mind. Traveling through the ether was not something she could even consider. It had felt alien and scary when Dagda took her. So, if not the ether then what? Train, plane? Where did he live and how far away was it really? She suddenly hoped for Jones. He could help her—and she knew if she worked her magic on him, he would. Was he still watching her? Knowing Dagda, he probably was.

Kat headed out early the next morning, her heavy down coat keeping out the cold. She figured if she wandered randomly, she might catch a glimpse of Jones. At least it wasn't raining today, although the wind was shredding the clouds and scattering them in all directions. She set off in the direction of the shop and then veered down an alley. Maybe if he thought she was up to something he'd follow a bit closer. She veered in and out of corners, stopping by a dumpster and then breaking into a run as she exited the alley. She glanced quickly over her shoulder, sure that she'd seen a shadow, but she didn't see him behind her. He must have private eye training.

An hour had gone by before she caught sight of him, his styled blonde hair disappearing behind a wall. Instead of thinking her way through it, she let her right brain take over, allowing a plan to rise to the surface. A few minutes later she let out a low chuckle and hurried toward where she'd last seen Jones. "Oh, hey!" she called out. "I thought that was you."

He turned, his face a mask of surprise. "What...?"

Before he could say another word, Kat was next to him, her hand gripping his arm. "That man you work for, Dagda? He's my father." He frowned and tried to jerk away, but she held firm. "I need to see him but I don't have the money to pay for a plane ticket and I don't have a driver's license. I want you to take me there—to his place of work."

"Does he know you're coming?"

She smiled sweetly. "It's a surprise."

Jones shook his head, a frown of confusion on his face. "I can't do that without his permission."

"Call him."

"You don't have his number, do you?" Jones asked, a simpering smile replacing his expression of confusion.

"No, but you do. I'll talk to him if you want me to. Just put in the damn number."

When Jones reached for his gun Kat had it out of his hand before he could take the safety off.

"What the fuck?" he yelled, wide-eyed.

"Call him," she said again, disengaging the safety.

He stared at her. "The guy'll kill me."

"No, he won't. He'll be happy to hear from me."

Jones let out a heavy sigh and pulled out his cell phone while Kat examined the alley they were in. The foot traffic on the main road was thin at this time of day, her anxiety about pointing a gun lessening. "Hurry up."

"I'm looking up his fucking number. I don't have him on speed dial."

She waited, watching him suspiciously until he began punching in numbers. When it began to ring he handed it over. "You talk to him."

"What is it, Jones?" Dagda's gruff voice asked.

"Hi Dad, it's me. Jones and I are here together in this alley. I have his gun pointed at him at the moment. He's promised to bring me to your office."

"Give the fucking phone to Jones!" he bellowed.

She handed it over. "He wants to talk to you."

"What the fuck, Jones? You let her find you? How stupid are you? I want you back here pronto, sans Katel. Do you understand?"

"What does sans mean?"

"It means *without*, you moron!"

"But she's got a gun, sir."

"Get the gun away from her…what are you, some stupid schoolboy in short pants?"

Kat heard every word Dagda said, laughter bubbling up as Jones ended the call. "That went well. Now how do we get to him?"

Jones glared at her. "You can't get away with this. Once we leave this alley there's no more gun pointing—you know that, right?"

Kat smiled. A second later the gun was invisible, Jones' scornful look turning to fear. Kat pushed him forward with the unseen barrel. "Lead the way."

A private plane was waiting at the airport, Jones discussing an itinerary with the pilot as Kat stood by. An hour later they were in the air, flying to the West coast city where Dagda lived. "Pasadena is a smallish city, but most of the people who live there come from wealth—many moved there from the east coast years ago," Jones told her conversationally.

"What does my father do, exactly?"

Jones snorted. "Hell, if I know. He runs a commercial real estate conglomerate, but there's more to it than that."

"I can imagine," Kat muttered, envisioning what Dagda had going for himself.

The building that housed Dagda's multiple businesses was taller than other buildings in the area, but not as tall as she would have thought. It was brick like the others, and beautifully constructed, with curved doors and windows and an air of old money. By this time the gun was empty and back in Jones's holster, his expression rigid as they stepped into the elevator. "I'm sure he's going to fire me," he muttered as the doors closed.

"Maybe not," Kat answered, glancing at him. The elevator stopped on floor thirteen, the doors hissing open.

Jones gave her a scathing look before heading into the glass fronted office. "Follow me."

"I'll just announce you," the older woman at the desk said once they'd entered the outer office. Prints of sailboats and antique cars lined the walls, the rich maroon carpet thick and sumptuous under their feet. The woman spoke into a phone and then gestured for them to wait in the leather chairs along one wall.

After five minutes Kat got up. "Where are you going?" Jones asked, reaching for her. But she was already halfway to the heavy mahogany door. A second later she'd turned the knob and entered, despite the shrill calls from the secretary.

Instead of sitting at the enormous desk, Dagda had his

back to the door, gazing out the enormous picture window. He turned when he heard the door, a deep frown on his features. "What happened to Beatrice?"

"Hello, *Dad*," Kat said, heading toward him. "I bypassed her."

His eyes narrowed. "Who exactly do you think you are?"

"I'm your daughter, doesn't that give me the right to visit?"

He stepped toward her. "This is outrageous. What do you expect to accomplish here?"

"I actually thought you could help me. I'm discovering some new abilities, and since Airmid and Gwen think I don't have any powers at all, I thought perhaps you could mentor me."

Dagda stopped in his tracks, his face going still. "Mentor…you expect me to mentor you? I thought you hated me."

"It's a love hate relationship, wouldn't you say? I expect you're not so fond of me right now, especially since I just outwitted your idiot PI and got him to fly me here."

"He's not long for this world."

"I hope you don't mean you'll kill him over this."

"More like fire his ass." He stepped behind his desk and sat heavily. "Your mother has been after me to set up another visit."

"Well, here I am."

"Yes, here you are. Since you seem to be running things, what now?"

"I want to know what to expect and how to handle it."

"I assume you're talking about your status as a goddess." He ran a hand across his face. "I'm not sure I can help you there—from what I've observed, you are quite unique."

Kat pulled a chair up to his desk. "You think I'm unique?"

Dagda nodded, an uneasy look on his face. "Nothing I've discovered about you is normal. I do not know any god or goddess who can manipulate the weather the way you do. These are things you need to understand and control, Katel. You could cause a catastrophe with your mood swings."

Kat choked as fear rose into her throat.

Dagda stared at her. "I thought you would be my undoing."

Kat coughed and breathed in and out before she answered. "Maybe I will be. Your actions are causing anomalies. If you don't go back to Otherworld both places could end up being taken over by those horrible Dubh creatures."

"You know about the Dubh?"

"I saw them in the forest when I was with Airmid. She said they steal the light. The forest was dead, Dad. It was gray and really creepy."

Dagda sighed. "I wish I could help, but I can't leave your mother."

"There has to be a way to get rid of them."

"If you have a suggestion, I'm all ears."

"You're the one who caused it! You have to be the one to fix it."

He shook his shaggy head. "I've come up with every scenario I can think of—short of me standing trial, there is nothing." He picked up his phone. "I'll have my driver take you to the house."

"Do you plan to hurt me?"

He paused with the phone in his hand. "If I hurt you, your mother would kill me."

That did little to make Kat feel better about his animosity toward her, but at least she knew she had leverage. An uneasy truce was better than no truce.

24

Once he arranged for Kat to be taken to the house, Dagda paced, his mind barely able to cope with what was happening. His daughter had outwitted the man he'd sent to tail her, and managed to get through his concealment spells to his office. In spite of a part of him being proud of her, he was also aware that he was now vulnerable. She could tell any one of the many gods trying to find him, where he was. He slammed his fist down on the desk and uttered an oath under his breath. If he had known what hell he'd have to pay from this one canny girl, he never would have brought her into the world. But back then he hadn't been thinking straight, his entire being devoted to Siobhan. When she became pregnant, he'd been overjoyed, hardly able to believe it. At least back then he'd had the sense to return to his life as a god.

None of this would have happened if he hadn't decided to bring Siobhan back from the dead. But when he imagined life without her his insides twisted. And they had a baby boy now. There was no going back. As far as saving the world from the light snatchers, there had to be another way.

He threw the door to his office open, surprised to see Jones sitting there. "What in hell are you doing here?"

"Waiting for your instructions?"

"Get out of my sight," he growled. "You are no longer in my employ."

Jones blanched and stood. "She's really fast. It wasn't my fault. She's a witch, sir, she made the gun invisible."

Dagda laughed. "You do know this is my daughter you're maligning?" He shook his head and walked past him, heading into the other offices to discuss the latest business debacle. Apparently there'd been an investigation into one of his companies that had revealed his illegal dealings. Now he had to bribe the officials to let it go. Either that or sic his daughter on them, he thought with a wry smile.

When he got home that evening Katel and Siobhan were in the living room with the baby, as thick as thieves. He tried not to appear as troubled as he felt, but the unexpected turn of events had left him shaken. Siobhan rose and greeted him as always, but there was a new expression in her eyes, as though her daughter had claimed a part of her heart formerly reserved for him.

"I ordered take-out," Siobhan said, after giving him a quick kiss.

"I need to talk to you," he hissed, attempting to tug her from the room.

She pulled free and went back to sit on the floor next to Mior and Kat. "We can talk later," she answered, turning to her daughter.

"I'll just take a shower," he said, waiting for her to offer to take one with him, one of their nightly rituals that he had grown especially fond of. But she just nodded and waved him away.

In the shower he thought about how to handle this new reality. "Maybe I should just hire her," he said out loud. "That way I can keep a close eye on her." But the idea of Kat moving in with them gave him a very queer feeling. He didn't want to share his wife with her. They had very few friends, and those they did have were on his terms only. Siobhan was there for him, not for anyone else. Maybe he could find an apartment for Kat, one close enough to his building so that she could walk to work. Would she be interested in what he had to offer? What would be her title, her duties? He thought about that for a while as he shampooed his hair, coming up with a new position, one that would utilize her emerging powers. She would be the liaison between him and all his businesses, especially the ones in which he was double dealing. She could navigate the thin line between illegal and legal practices and have a few face-to-face meetings with the ones who were threatening him. He knew who they were. If she objected to his nefarious activities, he would threaten to cut her off from Siobhan and the baby—at least he had that much power.

He turned off the shower and grabbed a towel, rubbing it vigorously over his wet hair before tying it around his waist. He ran his hand across the fogged mirror, gazing at his face. He looked tired and worn-out. These past few weeks had taken it out of him.

"How would you like to work for me?" he asked Kat after they'd eaten the Chinese food his wife had ordered.

She paused with her chopsticks in the air. "Doing what?"

He smiled. "I have a position I think you might enjoy. Perhaps tomorrow you can accompany me to work and we can go over the parameters."

"She will stay here with us, won't she?" Siobhan asked.

Dagda glanced at his wife and then back at his daughter. "I think Katel might be more comfortable closer to work. I know of a lovely condo in a building I own. She's a young woman, Siobhan, perhaps she would like to entertain a man occasionally?"

"Oh yes, of course," Siobhan agreed, looking crestfallen. "But we will see her on the weekends, right Katel?"

Kat nodded, an uncertain expression on her face as she glanced from one to the other.

Dagda watched the two of them, some buried emotion threatening to break loose. He was not used to these flashes that he couldn't control, sensations that ran through him like lightning, taking away who he was for that one blinding instant. *Damn it all,* he thought to himself. *I am a god and I am in control of this situation.* But some part of him denied that, a weakness penetrating his mind like a wall that was being broken down, brick by brick.

25

K at was at home in her apartment, her insistence on getting things organized in her own life seeming to take Dagda by surprise. "What did you think?" she'd yelled at him that morning in his office. "That I would come with the clothes on my back and just move in?"

"Go," he'd said, waving her away. "The plane is at your disposal, as is my driver. Take your time."

"You haven't exactly explained what my duties will be. You do know that I'm not versed in business practices or legal stuff, right?"

"You don't need to be. What I want from you is your sleight of hand."

"I don't know if I'd call it that, but whatever," she'd responded.

She looked around her apartment, trying to decide what to bring along. She needed to tell the landlord she was leaving, as well as Gwen, who had been handling the rent. When her gaze landed on her Celtic pendant on top of her chest of drawers, she picked it up, her mind going to Bran as it always did whenever she touched the antique piece. "I should give it back to Mom," she said to herself. But she'd grown very fond of it, especially since Bran had one very nearly identical to hers.

She felt the familiar buzz it always gave off, her fingers working across the silver as Bran arrived in her mind. But instead of the man she knew she saw a thin drawn face with a thick beard, his long unkempt hair tangled past his shoulders. The pendant around his neck shown dull silver in the pale light of wherever he was, and his eyes were sunken and dark, a defeated look in them she'd never seen before. She let out a gasp and dropped the pendant, hearing it clatter to the floor. "Where are you?" she whispered. "What has happened to you?" A second later she saw an ice-covered landscape of such utter desolation that she let out a little cry. A pain shot through her heart, an arrow that pierced her to her core. "I have to find you," she muttered. But how?

She called the shop on her cell phone, hoping to reach Gwen, but it went straight to voice mail. *Guess they've closed it up,* she thought to herself. *There's no reason for it now that my memories have returned.* Leaving the apartment without talking to Gwen would be fine, since the older woman had used magic on the landlord. But she would have preferred to say goodbye. She left a message saying she was moving and to please do whatever was necessary about the apartment and the things she left behind. She was still miffed about the two goddesses discussing her like she was some waif they'd picked up in an alleyway.

As she packed, she thought about Bran and how to go about finding him. Wherever he was, it was not on earth—

she was sure of that. Dagda would know, but she had the feeling if she mentioned Bran, he'd go ballistic. He didn't like the protection god, and since Bran had been the one to tell her who she really was, Kat was sure Dagda would like to see him obliterated.

It was late afternoon before she was ready to head to the airport where Dagda had left his private plane on stand-by. All she needed to do now was hire an Uber to get her there. Coast to coast in the Lear jet would take less than five hours. She would be in Pasadena by eight o'clock tonight California time.

Her shaking fingers pressed in the numbers for an Uber, her mind unable to cope with the new reality unfolding in front of her eyes.

The plane ride was bumpy, her adrenaline surging every time it lurched up or down. By the time they reached the airport she felt sick and exhausted. Instead of the inclement weather she'd left behind, the sky was dark and cloudless, stars visible and a balmy breeze blowing. Her spirits lifted. She found Dagda's dark blue Mercedes waiting at the curb and climbed in, stowing her small suitcase next to her.

"Is that all your luggage, miss?" the driver asked, surprised.

"Not sure how long I'll be staying," she answered, wondering why she hadn't thought to pack more. When she glanced out the window at the pedestrians her clothes seemed wrong, too dark and not suited for this climate.

Instead of taking her to the condo as Kat had been expecting, Daniel drove straight to Dagda's house, his automatic button allowing the gates to swing open, admitting the car into the property. He brought the Mercedes to a stop in front of the wide oak entrance and hopped out to open her door. Before she had a chance to grab it herself, he'd taken hold of her small suitcase, allowing her to precede him to the front door. A moment later a uniformed dark-skinned maid opened the door.

Siobhan hurried behind her, a wide smile of welcome on her face. "This is Lily, Lily this is my daughter, Katel," she said, before pulling Kat into a hug. "Dag insisted," she whispered. "He thinks I'm doing too much."

After releasing her, Siobhan reached to take Kat's bag from Daniel, but before she could get to it, Lily grabbed it and hurried away. "See what I mean?" she said, rolling her eyes.

"Where's Dad?"

"He had a late meeting tonight. I don't expect him until after we're both asleep."

"I thought he'd arranged a condo for me. I hate to put you out."

Siobhan made a sound in the back of her throat. "This house is enormous. If I had my way, you'd be living here with us. As to tonight, I insisted." She led the way up the wide stairs, following the maid who was already at the top and heading down a long hallway. "You'll be in the suite at the end of the hall. It faces the garden and has a spectacular view."

"Thanks," Kat mumbled, suddenly shy.

The room was spacious with a sitting room attached as

well as a marble bathroom with the biggest tub she'd ever seen. The bed was a king, the heavy posts carved into ravens. "Dad does like the ravens, doesn't he?"

Siobhan smiled. "He is a raven, you know."

"Just like Bran," Kat muttered.

"Bran? Yes, the god of protection who Dagda seems to take issue with."

"We love each other."

Siobhan's eyebrows rose. "You and Bran the blessed?" When Kat nodded, she continued. "I didn't meet him, but he was at the castle before we arrived—Odin's castle," she explained.

Kat turned from where she was examining the room. "Bran was there?"

"I overheard Frigg and Odin speaking about it. Apparently he told them a lot of things about Dag that upset them."

"You mean what his being on earth is doing to the world?"

"When I asked him about it, he denied it. He told me it's all a ploy to ruin his life."

Kat kept her mouth shut, not wanting a repeat of the fainting. "Where is Bran now?" she asked, her fingers going to the pendant around her neck.

Siobhan delicately raised one shoulder. "I don't know, but it seemed from what I overheard that he was on some kind of walk-about."

"Walk-about? You mean what the Australian aborigines do?"

"I suppose so." She glanced around the sumptuous room. "There are towels in the bathroom, and I've left you a pitcher of ice water and some cookies. Are you hungry for a real meal?"

"No. The plane ride made me feel a bit sick."

"I'm sorry, dear. You'll be ready for a nice breakfast after you've had a good sleep." She turned to leave and then stopped. "This love between you two, is it serious?"

"It was…Bran is the one who told me who told me who I really am. I think that's why Dad doesn't like him."

"Why would your father want to keep that from you?"

Kat stared at her, wondering how she could be so naïve. Instead of answering she just shrugged and turned away. They'd already discussed all this—had Dagda done some kind of magic on her again? When the baby let out a thin wail, Siobhan hurried from the room. "Like clockwork," she said over her shoulder.

Kat woke to sunlight pouring through her open window, drenching the room in golden light. She caught the scent of roses, and the tang of citrus flowers. She'd slept hard but managed to have nightmares about Bran, his haggard face still in her mind. She rose and went to the window, looking down on the garden. Instead of bare trees and bushes devoid of bloom or leaf, the place was filled with color. Bottle brush and other west coast plants vied for the most gorgeous honor, the garden ablaze with the early morning sunlight. Hummingbirds flitted here and there, something shifting inside her when she saw them. *Do I know you?* she wanted to ask. She heard voices coming from downstairs, Dagda's among them. "She needs her own place, Siobhan. I told you this already."

"But I've missed her so, and she could help with the baby."

"I hired Lily for all that. Katel will be working for me."

"She mentioned Bran last night. Do you know where he is?"

"No!" her father roared. "He is not good enough for her."

"She said they loved each other."

"I have at least two suitors in mind for her, Siobhan. Please don't encourage her in these meanderings. Hopefully Bran is gone for good."

When their voices faded Kat turned away, her heart pounding. Had Dagda arranged for Bran to be hurt in some way—was that why he looked so haggard and bereft in her visions? She pulled out a pair of jeans and a light sweater and dressed hurriedly.

The table in the dining room was filled with covered dishes, Siobhan and Dagda already seated with plates of eggs, bacon, fruit and toast in front of them.

"Help yourself," Siobhan invited, "and then come sit next to me."

"Good morning, Katel," Dagda said formally, a frown on his face.

"Hi *Dad*," she responded sarcastically.

"What is with you two?" Siobhan asked, staring from one to the other.

Dagda snorted. "I fear my daughter and I are too much alike."

"Not true," Kat said, helping herself to the perfectly scrambled eggs and a piece of thick-sliced homemade toast. She sat demurely next to her mother and tried not to look at Dagda who she could feel glaring at her.

"You're coming to work with me today," he announced, rising from the head of the table. "So, don't dawdle." He strode off.

"My goodness he's in a mood this morning," Siobhan said, shaking her head.

"Even before I got here?"

"Yes. He woke in a black mood and it seems to be continuing. I'm sorry he expects you to accompany him today. I was hoping for more time together. Will you come back for another night?"

"It's up to him," Kat said, tucking into her food.

Forty-five minutes later she was in the back of the Mercedes next to Dagda as Daniel navigated the crowded streets. Dagda glanced at her pendant, his eyes narrowing. "I gave that to your mother."

Kat turned from her perusal of the high-end shops, the richly dressed pedestrians, and the amazing bushes and trees planted in the middle of the wide road. "And she gave it to me."

"Give it back to her," he ordered, turning to stare out his window.

"I'm sure she'll refuse it."

He turned, his dark gaze meeting hers. "It was like a wedding ring, Katel. We didn't marry that time around."

"And you did this time?"

"Yes. We had a ceremony on the property right after I bought the house."

Kat wound her fingers around the pendant. "And who attended?"

"All my business associates and the people who work for me—a few friends."

"That must have been fun for her."

Dagda glared at her. "Your mother loved every minute of it."

"I'm sure she did."

"That smart mouth of yours is going to get you in trouble," he muttered, turning away.

Kat smiled to herself, glad that she'd touched a nerve. If he thought she was going to be crushed under his bootheel he was sadly mistaken.

"You will be doing some traveling," Dagda told her later in his office.

Kat turned from gazing out over the cityscape, in awe of the beauty of the place. "To where?"

"Where my business takes you. I have connections in Japan, in Hong Kong and in several other countries."

Kat moved to the chair in front of his desk. "I don't know what you expect of me. I don't speak any languages aside from English, and I've never had a job other than working in a shop or selling cardboard boxes."

Dagda smiled. "But you have qualities that are undeniable, ones which will work well to convince my competitors and my underlings that they will need to do exactly what I ask or face the consequences."

Kat frowned. "What kind of businesses are we talking about? I thought you were in commercial real estate."

"It's a lot more than that—and as my daughter you will oversee the more nefarious parts of it."

"Illegal stuff? What if I don't want to?"

Dagda narrowed his eyes. "If you know what's good for you, you'll do as I ask, Katel."

"Or? What will happen, *Dad?*"

"I can make your life very difficult."

"As though you haven't already. I'm immune to your bullshit now—you know that, right?"

"Your boyfriend isn't."

Kat stared at him. "What boyfriend are we talking about?"

"Bran. I know where he is and I can hurt him."

Kat shook her head and looked away, her heart speeding up. "I doubt that," she muttered to herself.

"Do not underestimate me. You may be stronger than I once thought, but I am still a god, and you have not yet tested all my powers."

"So, where is he?"

"He's in the Norse realm of Nifleheim near death. But don't let that influence you."

Kat rose quickly to her feet. "How do you know?"

"Frigg told me. She and I are very close."

"Frigg as in Odin's wife? Does Mom know?"

"Frigg tended your mother during the birth and afterward—of course she knows."

Kat sat heavily, feeling like a balloon that had just lost all its air. She didn't know if he was bluffing or not, but she didn't want to chance it; she'd seen visions of Bran's hollow-eyed face too many times recently. "Tell me exactly what you want me to do," she said in a small voice.

Dagda and Kat were on his private jet on their way to Hong Kong, his notes spread out on the table where they were sitting. "You will have to keep your wits about you with this particular man. He's sharp and he's been embezzling from me. I want you to stop him."

Kat looked up from the notes regarding this part of Dagda's business, her mind whirling with scattered facts and duplicities that she couldn't keep straight. "How do I do that?" she asked bluntly.

He shook his head, gazing at her silently. "Use your creativity, Katel. More than likely scaring the crap out of him will do the job."

"So, let him know that you know, and then...?" She threw her hands up in the air, "what?"

"You'll figure it out when the time comes."

"The trouble is most of what I do seems to arrive on its own because of need or fear."

"The person I plan to introduce you to will literally stab you in the back—is that enough fear for you?"

Kat went cold all over. She pulled her sweater close and

stared into space, listening to the drone of the engines. When she spoke again her bravado had simply disappeared. "I do not feel confident about this—he's a criminal. I've never dealt with criminals. What if nothing comes to me? I can't just be standing there like an ineffectual idiot."

Dagda gazed at her blandly. "You stood up to me and I'm a god. Do you really think you can't stand up to a normal human being?"

"Why don't you do it?"

"Because I want to turn this part of things over to you. I have enough going on in other aspects of the business. This is a dry run. If things go well, I'll set you loose on others who are cheating me."

"How did you get all these businesses set up so quickly?"

Dagda snorted. "How do you think?"

When they landed in Hong Kong hours later Kat noticed the mountains of green in the distance that lay impassive, like some sort of sleeping beast. But she also saw the colorless gray haze of the Dubh. When she turned to mention it to Dagda, he was already striding down the aisle with his briefcase. Her main impression as they'd flown in was a clustered mass of high-rises. She patted the money belt her father had insisted she wear under her clothes, where her passport, and the thousands of dollars he'd foisted on her, were tucked away. She had no idea why he'd been so adamant about her having so much money, but she didn't argue.

"Before we go to the hotel, we need to pay my manager a little visit," Dagda told her once they left the airport. He led the way to a waiting a car and the man behind the wheel who was obviously his private driver. "Once you've straightened Liu out, I'll pick you up and we can go and check in," he continued as they stowed their bags and climbed into the car. "I know you're tired Katel, but first things first, I'm afraid."

Kat glanced at him. It was the first caring thing he'd said to her in two days.

Kat rubbed her tired eyes, trying to focus on the small man in front of her. Liu was narrow-eyed with straight coal black hair, a shifty expression on his features. Dagda had dropped her off in an enormous warehouse and taken off to do some other business that he didn't explain.

"What you want with me?" he asked her, watching Dagda drive away.

"My father seems to think you've been double-dealing," she answered, modulating her voice. There were other men around and a warehouse full of boxes behind her, their contents unknown. If any one of those muscly men made a move, she wasn't sure what she would do.

"No double deal. Honest deal. Your father knows."

"Can I see your receipts for the past few months please?"

A frown appeared on his face. "Receipt book in safe."

"I don't care where they are, I need to see them."

He shook his head and led the way toward the back of the cavernous room and headed up a set of rickety metal stairs. Kat followed him into a glass fronted office, watching him nod to the dark-haired Chinese woman sitting at a desk. When he spoke to her in rapid Mandarin she turned to stare malevolently at Kat. It was obvious that he'd told her that Kat was there to catch them in whatever game they'd been playing. A second later she rose and hurried through a door, returning a moment later with a box of files.

"Here is books," Liu said, gesturing for her to examine the files.

Kat shook her head. "I don't read Mandarin, nor do I speak it."

"Why you here? Dagda know language and how to read too."

Kat breathed in and out slowly, trying to figure out what to do. If Dagda knew the man was cheating then it wouldn't matter what she found in the files—he would have hidden it. "Can we speak privately please?" she asked him.

He turned and opened the door into another room and she followed, carrying the box with her. "Please sit," she said once they were inside the windowless room with the door closed. She placed the file box on the table, waiting as he pulled up a chair. Nothing came to her for several drawn-out moments until she had a vision of what was in the boxes downstairs. They were filled with illegal drugs and weaponry, her father's side businesses. An image of three men dying in a back alley came to her and another of several dark-haired women and men lying on stained mattresses as their eyes closed for the final time. She saw people shooting each other, blood and chaos—she heard their screams. She felt sick to her stomach, gagging as she held down bile. This man was responsible for so much death, but her father was too—her father had started this business. Liu was cheating him, but it didn't really matter—death was the result, no matter what was going on. "You will stop cheating my father," she said in a low voice. "If you do not, he will kill you."

When Liu scoffed and attempted to stand up, Kat waved her hand, sending him heavily back into the chair. His eyes widened in fear. "Why you think I cheat? I not cheat."

"If Dagda says you're cheating, then you are. He knows, Liu. He knows everything. What I want you to do is get rid of those boxes downstairs. Throw them in the river. They are contraband."

"But…Dagda, he say send out. We have contract. If not follow through then…" he made a slicing gesture with his hand along his neck.

Kat imagined the downstairs, visualized the stacked boxes bursting into flames. A second later she heard shouting and smelled smoke. And a moment after that explosions reverberated, shaking the building. Liu was up and running, his face pale as he flung open the door and pelted down the stairs. She heard shouts and men's voices, metal rattling as people ran up the stairs. She saw them in her mind's eyes, guns drawn, looking for her.

Kat moved into the other office, searching for another way out. The Chinese woman was gone, papers scattered across her desk. A small window caught Kat's eye and she shoved it open and stood on a chair to pull herself up. But it was too small an opening. She was desperate now, the men almost upon her and the smoke filling the office making her eyes water. Before she could think what to do, something began to happen to her body, her limbs shrinking away, everything compacting. Her consciousness shrank along with it, a kaleidoscope of colors shifting in the ultraviolet world around her. She felt rather than saw gossamer wings, the sound of their high-speed movement penetrating into the part of her mind that still clung to Kat, the woman. Less than a second later she was airborne, lifting on the thermals that eddied around the building from the fire. Her bird mind heard the explosions, her instinct to get as far away from here as possible. She lifted high into the air and flew.

Red, she saw all shades of red, from pale pink to deep magenta, oranges and pale lilac—hollyhocks, daylilies, petunia, foxglove, trumpet vine. She drank from a flower, her narrow beak deep inside to reach the nectar. Some had less, some had more—she moved from one bush to another, searching, always searching. There were bugs along the way, succulent, juicy, filled with what she needed. Where she was going was not part of her consciousness, the only thing she knew was to search for food.

27

K at came back to herself a long time later, unsure exactly what had happened. She was in a forest of pine and palms and other trees she didn't know the names of. Monkeys chattered, their beady eyes watching her as she stood and dusted herself off. The scent of jungle came to her, the understory of thick-leafed bushes, and the ripe smell of rotting fruit overwhelming her senses. Bananas had been thrown away, either that or they grew here and the monkeys had brought them. But then she saw the banana plants, the deep purple flower that she hazily remembered as something that had attracted her to this place.

Her trip from plant to plant came back to her in vague detail, her flight haphazard and driven only be the vibrant infrared colors. A second later her legs gave out and she landed on her backside, the realization of what had happened sending shockwaves through her body. She leaned against the trunk of a tall and very straight pine, running through the events of the day and this latest revelation. Apparently, she could turn into a bird, a hummingbird, to be exact.

She was dozing when she had the memory about her seven-year-old self. It was during the time when she and her mother lived in the commune. Kat had been out playing alone in the woods, as she did nearly every day, when she turned into a hummingbird. Back then it had seemed perfectly natural, as though everyone could do it, just a part of everyday life. She distinctly remembered the feeling of it all, the way her vision changed and the ability to fly straight up and backwards, and to dive down at an unbelievable speed. But when she mentioned the experience to her mom, Siobhan had laughed, not meanly, but Kat knew her mom thought she was making it up. Somehow her mother's derision made her feel that maybe she *was* making it all up, despite the amazing way she'd been able to see and hear, and the flowers she drank from. She'd stopped doing it and put the experience out of her mind and never thought of it again. Until today.

It was getting dark by the time Kat roused herself from her reverie and decided to make a plan. She still had her money belt and the cash Dagda had given her, more than enough to buy a plane ticket back to the U.S. This new and wondrous talent of hers would be kept secret. Dagda did not need to know. He would be furious as soon as he found out what she'd done at the warehouse—maybe he already knew and had sent out scouts to find her…right now she had to locate the road, hail a taxi and get herself to the airport before he found her.

Kat was boarding when she caught sight of Dagda rushing up to the ticket counter, his hands lulling everyone into a stupor. She hurried down the boarding bridge, hoping he hadn't seen her. She was on pins and needles until the doors closed, only letting out her held breath when they began to taxi down the runway.

Kat woke to a very different world, the plane landing in Pasadena where beautiful mansions outnumbered the commercial buildings. During the long plane ride she'd thought long and hard about her next move, her first inclination to fly to the east coast instead of the west. But she wanted to see her mother before she made a final decision.

The only thing she knew for sure was that she wanted to stay as far away from Dagda and his double-dealing as possible. Even now the visions of people dying as a result of his drugs and guns made her feel ill. Her original thought of being able to keep an eye on him by working for him had changed.

The taxi took her directly to Dagda's house where she climbed out, paid the driver and pressed the intercom.

"Kat! What has happened? Why are you here? Your father called last night to tell me that you'd disappeared."

Kat threw herself onto the sofa. "He's a crook, Mom. He's got a legitimate business that he's using to run illegal drugs and arms. He's a monster."

Siobhan's eyes widened before she sat next to her daughter. "That can't be. He knows how I feel about such things."

Kat pushed herself up. "I had a vision of what happens

to the people who end up using his wares, and it is not a pretty sight."

Siobhan shook her head, frowning. "No, Katel. You must be mistaken. I told him years ago…when we were together the first time, how I felt about illegal drugs and also about weapons. He can't…he wouldn't…"

Kat let out a heavy sigh. "And yet he is. He wanted me to scare his manager who he thinks is embezzling from him. But while I was there, I figured out that the warehouse was packed with boxes of opioids and weapons. I burned it down."

"Ah, that's what he meant when he told me that our daughter had taken matters into her own hands."

"And did he mention why I might do that?"

"He said you'd disobeyed him and run off."

"True—that's true."

Siobhan gazed out the window, her forehead puckered in a frown of worry. "What do I do now?" she whispered. "If he's truly doing these things, then I…" She turned to face Kat. "I can't stay with him. But how on earth can I leave? I'm his creation, Kat, and we have a child together."

"Come with me, Mom. We can find a place to live, and…"

Siobhan shook her head. "No. I can't do that. I will speak to him when he comes home."

"So, you'll believe what he has to say over what I've just told you?"

"I didn't say that. But I can't leave him without discussing it. He may have a very good explanation."

"And a lot of magic to get you to see it his way," Kat muttered, standing.

"No dear, he doesn't use magic on me."

"The hell he doesn't." Kat glanced around the room, her mind reeling with the plight of her mom and the treachery of her father. She *was* his creation—he could do whatever he wanted with her. But Dagda loved her. Kat had seen it. And they had a child together. Dagda certainly didn't feel any love toward Kat, his firstborn. "I have to go. I wish you and Mior would come with me."

"I wish you'd wait for your father to return. He told me he was taking the next flight out—he'll be here very soon."

Kat had a moment of panic. "I have to get out of here," she said urgently.

"Bye, Mom. I love you."

Siobhan pulled Kat close. "I don't want you to go," she whispered, tears welling.

Kat let herself be held, sadness welling up as she realized it might be a very long time before she saw her mom again. She thought about her baby brother, wishing she had the time to see Mior before she left, but Dagda could arrive any second. She pulled away and hurried toward the front door. "Kat...Kat!" she heard her mom cry out, but she didn't look back.

When Kat headed out the front door, the blue Mercedes was arriving, adrenaline sending her into panic mode. But instead of turning back to find another way out of the garden, the transformation came over her, what was left of her human mind hoping that Dagda had not been looking in her direction. A moment later she was whirring around the garden, sampling the flowers in preparation for what she knew, even in her hummingbird mind, would be a very long trip. The knotted tangle of confusion had been replaced with an all-knowing instinct that propelled her forward.

28

"**K**atel is out of control, Siobhan! Do not blame this on me!" Dagda roared, making the glassware on the shelf rattle.

"She said you're doing criminal things, Dag—selling illegal drugs and guns."

Dagda's hands turned into fists. "All the gods damn it! That girl better hide, or I'll…"

"You'll what? Would you hurt our daughter? If she's telling the truth I can't stay here."

Dagda stared at her in horror. "You have to stay. I can't live without you. And…" He stared off, his eyes turning opaque.

"And…you made me what I am? In all honesty, if what she said is true, I'd rather you'd never brought me back from the dead."

"I gave you *life*, Siobhan, and a baby. Isn't that enough? And where did she go so fast? Didn't you say she was leaving just as I arrived? I never saw her."

"Maybe she walked down the hill? I don't know. But I do know she was very upset."

When Siobhan turned away, hurrying up the stairs to

retrieve the crying baby, Dagda paced, his brow furrowed in anger. He should never have trusted Kat. Not only had she destroyed millions of dollars worth of inventory, she was also trying to destroy his life. Where in hell had she gone so quickly?

Siobhan treated him like a pariah the entire night, her focus solely on the baby as he tried to reason with her about his feelings. By the time they went to bed he was beside himself with frustration, her rejection of his advances the last straw. In the two lives they'd been together she'd never once turned him down, even after arguing.

In the morning Dagda and Siobhan had another knock down drag out fight, one in which he couldn't stop himself from taking one step further, his cocktail of shouted words laced with vitriol. She was crying when he left, her face red and swollen as he stomped out the door to the car and Daniel.

"Is everything all right, sir?" the driver asked.

"No, Daniel, it is not. But I hope to have things straightened out soon. By the way, did you happen to see my daughter leave the other day when you brought me home?"

"No, sir. I did see her come out the front door, but she must have walked around the back of the house."

"Was she carrying her suitcase?"

"Not that I saw."

Dagda was quiet for the rest of the trip, his anger and fear about the future filling him with black rage. His gut twisted like snakes caught in a vise, making him wish he was near a toilet. Was he becoming human on top of everything else? Kat was responsible for all of it, and she would pay.

At work he paced his office, at one point letting out a bellow of rage as his thoughts turned again to his daughter. A second later his door opened and Beatrice peeked inside.

"Do you need me, sir?"

"No…I mean yes, Beatrice. Please assemble my gang of eight for an after-lunch meeting."

"Yes, sir, right away." The door closed softly and he heard her dialing numbers. At least his hearing hadn't deteriorated, he thought, as he rushed to his adjoining bathroom. Returning to his desk he thought of his businesses, the world he'd created here. His daughter had put it all in jeopardy, including his relationship with Siobhan. He was now faced with a rock and a hard place, to use an idiom from this culture. Did he have to become human to satisfy his wife? Would she be happy living in a hovel somewhere? Of course she would, he realized. During his first life with her they'd lived in a commune for a while where she'd worn long gypsy skirts and gone barefoot most of the time. He'd loved that aspect of her. But this time—this time he'd created a world of luxury, hoping she would enjoy it. Did she? He honestly did not know.

He was staring out his picture window when Frigg entered his thoughts. He felt an urgent need to see her, knowing that out of everyone she would cut to the chase and know what he should do about the crumbling situation. He strode into the outer office and asked Beatrice to put the meeting off.

"But…I've already contacted six of them."

"Call them back and tell them I'll reschedule when I'm ready. Right now I have an errand to run."

"When will you be back, sir?"

He turned from the door into the outer hallway. "As soon as I can. But please hold all my meetings and calls until the day after tomorrow. I have a bit of traveling to do."

Traveling through the ether was satisfying after all his earthbound activities. His raven mind relished the wind ruffling through his feathers and he experienced the joy of rising on the thermals and dropping with his wings tucked before widening them out to lift once again. He was barely aware of time passing as he made the trip to the castle.

"What are you doing here?" Frigg hissed, pulling him from the front hall into the shadows.

"I need you, Frigg. I'm having a very bad time right now."

"I know that look, Dagda. I've seen it before. Is it only sex that you want or is it more serious?"

Dagda took hold of her arm and dragged her down the hallway, opening a door at random.

"Not here," Frigg said, pulling him out. "Hold tight," she ordered, taking the two of them through the ether to her private turret.

The room where they landed was round and filled with her apothecary supplies, the aroma of spice and herbs filling his senses. A narrow bed lay along one wall, covered in a hand-woven tapestry in purple and gold. "Odin never comes here so we'll be safe from prying eyes. Now what is it you need so desperately from me, or should I even ask?"

Dagda smiled. "Yes, that, but I also need advice." He took her face in his big hands and leaned down to place his lips on hers.

Frigg pulled away. "What is this advice you need, Dagda?"

Dagda let out a sigh and ran his fingers through his dark, tangled mass of hair. "I can't think right now—can we…"

Frigg let out a laugh. "You can't think until you've had your way with me?"

Dagda nodded, a sheepish grin arriving on his face.

Frigg stared at him unblinking. "I have to admit there's chemistry between us."

"In other words, you need it as much as I do?"

"Maybe not quite as much as you do, but yes. I haven't lain with a man or a god since the last time you were here."

Dagda tugged at her gown, his fingers clumsy. She pushed him away and removed it herself, standing before him in a gossamer shift that showed every curve and valley of her lush body. "Gods," he moaned, undoing the buttons on his trousers. He watched her pull the light shift over her head before he picked her up and carried her to the bed. His lips moved between her full breasts, his fingers working through her silky blonde hair as he kneeled over her. When she let out a moan, he entered her, watching her eyes turn opaque and then close, her lips slightly apart. He kissed her as he began to move, slowly at first until she lifted her hips to urge him on, adjusting his body to hers as she pulled him in deeper. They rocked together, their sighs and groans of pleasure mixing with the scents of sage and mint. He waited for her before he allowed himself to let go, a near shout exploding from him as he finished. He moved to lie next to her, pulling her close as they caught their breath.

"At least it wasn't violent this time," Frigg murmured.

They consummated their passion a second time before Frigg pushed herself up to sitting. "Are you ready to talk now, Dagda? I don't have all day to lie around in bed with you."

"Was it…was it good?"

Frigg chuckled. "The great Dagda needs assurances about his prowess as a lover? Wasn't it obvious?"

Dagda smiled for the first time. "Yes, I guess it was, especially since it was you who initiated the second time around."

"Me? No, that was your doing."

Dagda shook his head and pushed himself up to sit beside her. She was so different from Siobhan, her body full and rounded where Siobhan's was small-breasted with narrow hips. She was freer in bed, more expressive than Siobhan. He wasn't sure which type he liked more. "I do feel more like myself now."

"You mean thinking with that part of you has been taken out of the equation?"

He snorted. "It helps me get my head on straight, Frigg. And Siobhan—she hasn't let me touch her in days."

"Poor baby!" Frigg teased, reaching to touch his leg. He grabbed her and they tumbled for a moment until Frigg slapped his hand away. "No more of that. Now tell me the other part, the part you're trying to avoid."

He straightened and leaned back, a frown on his face as he thought of his wife, his daughter and the trouble Kat had caused. "Siobhan…Kat told her about my double-dealing—my illicit businesses."

Frigg laughed. "Did you think you could keep it secret from a smart and savvy woman like Siobhan?"

Dagda felt the anger rise, attempting to modulate his voice. "She wouldn't have known if Katel hadn't informed her. I hired Kat with the idea of…"

"And she turned on you, is that it? I'm not surprised after all she's been through. Did you expect her to run your illegal dealings?"

"Well, I…"

"Really, Dagda. For a god you certainly have a blind spot. Your daughter is Siobhan's daughter too. She has ethics and morality, unlike you, who has neither. This problem is of your own making."

"I know that, Frigg! Why do you think I'm here?" he roared.

Frigg raised her hand to shush him. "Keep your voice down. We are in my turret, but as you are well aware, gods have very acute hearing. What do you expect of me? I can't solve any of this."

"I just need advice on how to proceed."

Frigg glanced at him blandly. "As I see it you have two choices: keep your businesses going and lose Siobhan, or get rid of your businesses and make peace with your wife and go back to Otherworld where you belong."

"I can't let my business go—I'm in too deep. And Siobhan—I love her. Kat needs to pay for…"

"Dagda," Frigg said, rising from the bed to reach for her gown, "Kat is not your problem. Your problem is your unwillingness to see what you've done and are continuing to do. You're leading a false life in a world that is not your own. The Norse world, Otherworld, and earth are all suffering as a result of your actions. Will you let the light snatchers turn everything gray, or will you do the right thing?"

When Dagda arrived home that night the maid answered the door, her worried gaze meeting his. "Madame is gone," she said. "She took the baby and asked me to tell you she's leaving you."

Lily backed away when Dagda's hands turned into fists. "What else did she say? Who took her…Daniel? Where did she say she was going?"

"She didn't say, sir. She had a suitcase with her and I didn't see if the driver picked her up or not."

"You're fired!" he shouted, rushing up the stairs to their bedroom. Drawers had been left open, clothing strewn from one side to the other. In the bathroom all her personal things were gone. He let out a bellow of rage and ran his hand over any remaining bottles left on the bathroom granite, glass shattering as it hit the floor. A second later his hands went to cover his face where tears slid down, his desolation like nothing he'd ever experienced before.

29

Kat woke shivering, her eyes opening on a land of ice and fog. She had no idea how she'd arrived here, had only a vague memory of her bird mind fixed on this destination. But where was the destination? *Niflheim.* Dagda had mentioned Niflheim when he taunted her with the news of Bran being near death. She knew of Niflheim, had read about all the Norse realms back when she was in school, many of which would be a lot more hospitable than this freezing place. She shook with cold, her teeth chattering, a memory of frozen wings and plummeting to the ice going through her mind. If she hadn't turned into her human form, she'd be dead now, the tiny hummingbird heart unable to withstand such freezing temperatures.

In the distance she noticed an uneven range of blue-white, a mountain or a hill that interrupted the flatness of ice. If she were to find shelter of any kind it would be there, although how far away it lay was hard to determine. Despite her thirst and hollow belly Kat pushed herself up and began to walk toward that mirage-like vision. It felt like hours had gone by when she had the strange sense that nothing had changed; she was no closer to her goal than she had been when she began. Her eyes burned with fatigue as she bent to scrape through the ice, her fingers bleeding as she shoved the chips into her mouth. Her hands were blue, every part of her numb as she resumed her steady walking, the knowledge that she would be dead soon like a mantra that wouldn't let her go. Visions of being on horseback plagued her, images of riding next to Bran as though they were warriors on their way to battle, leaving her breathless. She'd never ridden a horse in her life.

Kat was curled on the ground feeling nothing but the blessed relief of being near death, when she heard the thump of something heavy landing next to her. She tried to open her eyes only to find they were frozen shut. Gentle hands warmed them until she was able to see, the sight before her making her wish her eyes were closed. A half woman half monster towered over her, one dark eye peering at her from the human side of her face. The other half was sinew and bone, a sight so hideous she had to turn away.

"What are you doing in my realm?" the creature asked.

"I...I don't know. Something must have drawn me here."

There was a snort of derision. "Nothing draws anything here," she scoffed. "This is Niflheim, the land of the unremembered dead. It is a place of corpses and cold."

Kat shivered violently, unable to respond for a moment as she tried to control her chattering teeth. "Bran..." she muttered. "Dagda said that Bran the blessed, was here," she managed.

"Bran, the blessed. Oh yes, he was here. Not sure if he succumbed to the elements or not."

"Where can I find him?"

"I have no idea, but there is a creature who might be able to help you. He lives there," she said, pointing a bony finger toward the mountain.

When Kat glanced in that direction it seemed that the mountain was closer than it had been. "This creature, is it like you?"

There was a mirthless laugh before she said, "I am the goddess Hel. There is no one like me. I am the product of my father, Loki."

"I may freeze before I get there," she muttered.

Hel peered at her. "You are a goddess. You must have some control over your fate here."

Kat opened her mouth to ask how Hel knew Kat was a goddess, and what she should do, but before the words formed Hel lifted into the air, her misshapen shadow sliding across the ice in the other direction.

I should have asked for food, Kat thought as her stomach turned in on itself. *I'll never make it that far without sustenance.* But then she thought of Niflheim being the land of corpses and thought better of it. A second after that Kat had a vision of Bran, his face haggard, cheeks sunken, his beautiful moss colored eyes filled with despair. She had no idea how she managed it, but a minute later she was up and running, her feet seeming to skim across the ice, her stride lengthening as she covered the distance that lay between her and the distant mountain.

It was close to dusk, if you could call the lowering pall that hung over the already dark sky, dusk. Kat was exhausted and starving, her limbs shaking with fatigue and cold. Any adrenaline she'd had was long gone. The mountain loomed in front of her, much larger than she'd originally thought. Its sides were slick with ice, dark slate appearing here and there like the underpinnings of some massive iron beast. The sky was nearly dark now, no stars to mar the absolute blackness that seemed to descend like a curtain. Kat scrabbled into fissures and crevasses trying to find a place out of the cold wind. Too tired to think or go a step further she fell into a deep and dreamless sleep.

It was later when the cold had brought her out of sleep, that she huddled and pushed down and down, attempting to find warmth where there was none. When her foot slipped, she had a moment of panic...the next thing she knew she was sliding down an ice shoot, her hands bloodied as she tried to stop her descent, or at least slow it. When she finally landed, she hit hard, her hip screaming in pain.

It took her a while before the pain let up enough to take a look around at where she was, her focus on the wide ledge leading off into the far distance. She heard a rumbling sound and then noticed a flicker of flame coming up from a dark hole about fifteen feet away. Warmth, was her first thought as she hurried closer, her feet sliding on the ice that had melted and then refrozen, leaving a slick veneer that almost took her down. The opening loomed ahead, the flames rising from it, periodic and accompanied by a sound very much like an outbreath. There was also a stench that had her gagging. "What is this?" she whispered, falling to her hands and knees to crawl closer.

"Who is there?" a low rumbling voice asked.

Kat stopped mid crawl. "I...I'm Katel. Who are you?"

There was a sound like a freight train rumbling in the distance. "I am Nidhogg."

"Nidhogg—should I know you?"

This time she recognized the laughter bubbling up. "I know who *you* are," he answered.

"How do you know me? I've never been here before—what are you, anyway?"

"I am a dragon, and the reason I know of you is because of Bran, who spent many hours extolling your virtues."

"Bran—you've seen him?"

"Of course, I have seen him. I just said so. He spent some time here with me."

Kat crawled to the edge of the narrow opening and peered downward, trying to see in the dim light. She could just make out the shape of him, his wings, and one yellow eye that peered up at her. "Where is he now?"

"How should I know? Hel rescued him and that was the last I saw of him."

"Hel…she's the creepy monster who…"

"I take issue with that description. Hel has kept me alive all these many centuries that I have been trapped in here."

"I'm sorry. She's just so…"

"She is in Niflheim because of others who could not stand to look upon her. I find it offensive that no one can see beneath the surface of things."

Kat felt suddenly ashamed of herself. "You're right. She's the one who pointed me here. But now I'm not sure what to do. Perhaps you can help me?"

"Did you not hear what I just said? I am a prisoner here."

Kat leaned closer, staring down into the pit and trying

to keep herself from sliding in. "How did that happen?"

There was a heavy sigh before a few flames wafted up and singed the ends of her hair. "I was young when Odin clipped my wings and cast me into this pit. Hel has kept me alive by feeding me the corpses that end up in this realm."

That was the reason for the horrible smell. "But why? What did you do to deserve such a fate?"

"I did not agree with the gods' decision to leave Loki's daughter here for all eternity."

Eternity—the word gave her a bad feeling. "Maybe I can release you. If I do, will you help me find Bran?"

"I would do anything to get out of this pit. So, the answer to your question is yes. But I also wonder how you will manage such a feat."

"I have been known to control the elements," she muttered.

"Speak up, girl. I thought I heard you say you can control the elements."

"I can conjure storms, or I should say it happened a couple of times when I got angry."

"Hmm…a storm will not help me. We have them here with alarming regularity and so far not one of them has deigned to release me from this prison."

"How about earthquakes?"

"Now that is an interesting idea, although it could cause the mountain to collapse in on me."

"Not if I'm down there with you. But how do I do that without killing myself?"

"I will stand underneath and you can drop onto my back."

Kat wondered—did she trust the dragon? He seemed

reasonable, but maybe he wanted to lure her down there to eat her.

"I know what you are thinking," he said. "But I only eat dead things."

"For all I know you'll move out of the way and I'll kill myself—and then you'll eat me."

"You are a goddess and have just told me you will release me from this pit I have been living in for centuries. Why would I choose to hurt you?"

Kat thought about turning into a hummingbird, quickly dismissing it when she took in a breath of frigid air. She would be dead before she flew into the pit. And if he was lying, he would eat her in whatever state she happened to be in. She leaned over the dark opening. "How far will I have to fall before I land on your back?"

Nidhogg chuckled. "Not far—I seem to have filled out the space. And if you do not land in the center of my back, I will move to make sure I catch you."

Kat sat back on her heels, her mind swirling in circles. Should she—shouldn't she? But then she thought of Bran and how Nidhogg had promised to help her find him. She had to trust someone, didn't she? She may as well start with a dragon. "Okay," she called out. "Get ready."

There was a shuffle and rumble as the dragon moved. "I am in place," he said a moment later.

Kat slid her legs over the edge, her heart pounding. "Are you right under the hole?"

"I can see your feet and legs. If you slide down you will land on the widest part of my back. My wings are out to catch you if you slide sideways."

Kat leaned forward, but was unable to see his wings. She

took a deep breath, pushed off with her hands, and let herself go. There was a horrible moment of empty air, darkness taking her sight. And then she landed on something bumpy and scaly, her hands going out to stop her fall. She needn't have bothered, the wings Nidhogg had mentioned curled around her to keep her safe. The smell was beyond horrible, her eyes watering as they adjusted. "How many decaying bodies do you have down here?" she asked, breathing through her mouth.

"What you are smelling is the hundreds of years of my feces and urine and the bones that might still have some flesh remaining. The sooner you work your magic the sooner we can both get out of here."

By this time Kat's eyes had adjusted, her gaze going to the piled skeletons that filled in the shadowy niches. Shuddering, she tried not to gag. The pit was enormous, which was good considering the mound of what she could only assume was the dragon's manure that stretched endlessly into the darkness. She held her nose as he bent to his knees to allow her to slide off.

"If you follow the cave back there you will find water," Nidhogg told her, gesturing to where the roof and walls narrowed. "The spring feeds Yddrassil's roots. There may be something green growing in the places where I can no longer reach. I assume you are hungry and thirsty."

"Yes," she replied, gazing up at his enormous bulk, the canny eye that watched her. He loomed more than ten feet above her, his scales gleaming dark green in the dim light. She was suddenly aware that her shivering had ceased. It was warm in here. The stench was nearly overpowering, but being warm lessened its effect on her.

"Go now and find what you need to keep yourself alive and then we will discuss the next step."

One of his wings pointed into the deeper part of the cave and Kat did what he suggested, hoping it wasn't a trap. So far he'd been nothing but helpful, but her trust was at an all-time low. All she could think of was Bran and finding him. According to Nidhogg Bran had left here alive. Was it possible he hadn't succumbed to the cold? In the back she cupped her hands and drank the frigid water, tasting the sweetness it held. And when she found the greens, she almost cried with joy.

Despite the driver assuring Dagda that not only had he not seen Siobhan, that if he had he would have alerted his boss, Dagda called him and read him the riot act. After hanging up Dagda berated Lily for letting Siobhan leave.

The maid had arrived in the hall with her small suitcase when Dagda started in, his voice echoing off the walls. "You should have contacted me immediately!" he shouted.

"But sir, she is a free and independent woman. I didn't know she was leaving you."

"The suitcase didn't give you a clue? How stupid are you? That's my baby she's taken along with her."

Lily's frightened eyes met his. "Does she have friends or relatives she might be visiting?"

Dagda shook his head, his agitated fingers running through his knotted hair. "The only person I can think of is Kat, our daughter, but I have no idea where she is and I'm sure Siobhan doesn't either…unless…did you hear her talking on the phone?"

"No sir. I was in the kitchen until she came to let me know she was leaving."

Dagda let out a heavy sigh and opened the door. "Go, he ordered, slamming the door as soon as she was on the other side.

Dagda paced up and down, his heavy steps leaving footprints in the lush hall carpeting, before he took his cell phone out and called her number. She'd been loath to have one, but he'd insisted. When he heard it ringing in the living room his heart sank. He had no means of getting in touch with her. *I'm a god*, he muttered to himself. *I found my daughter in the park, I can certainly find my wife and son. And when I do, they're coming home with me.*

When his cell phone rang in his pocket he grabbed it out and slid his finger across the screen, hoping it was Siobhan. Instead it was Beatrice, her distraught voice reverberating in his ear. "You've had several phone calls, sir, and an FBI agent came by this morning looking for you."

"What? What did you tell him?"

"It was a woman, and I told her that you weren't in yet. She insisted that I let you know she'd been here. 'A matter of the utmost urgency to discuss,' she said."

"Is she coming back?"

"I assume so, but she expects you to call her. I have the number here."

Dagda ended the call abruptly, his mind whirling. It seemed that his nefarious activities had come to the attention of authorities who he'd been hoping to elude. He felt the net closing in around him as he rushed out the door. A moment later he was a raven, his shape dark against the pale blue of the sky as he allowed his instincts to take over. In his raven mind he was looking for his mate and his offspring, and it was the single most important thing he'd ever done. In the distance he noticed the creeping gray where the color had been leeched out of the forest. Even as raven he knew this was not good.

He felt the pull of his mate, his wings closing so he could dive to where he'd felt her the strongest. As soon as he landed he was Dagda again, scanning the street where he'd felt her presence. She was heading into a coffee shop, the baby in her arms. He hurried after her.

When he entered the coffee shop Siobhan had her back to him, and was joining a blond-haired man in a booth. He could hear their conversation, detecting that this man was a lawyer and she was consulting him about getting a divorce.

Mior saw him first, letting out a gurgle as he recognized his father.

Siobhan turned, her eyes going wide as he approached the booth.

"What do you think you're doing?" he asked her.

"I'm filing for divorce."

"You can't divorce me, you know that, Siobhan."

The man sitting across from her frowned. "This is an uncontested divorce state."

"The hell it is. What if I don't agree?"

"It makes no difference if you agree or not. Your wife has the right to get a divorce, despite your feelings about it."

When Mior began to cry, Dagda reached for him. Reluctantly Siobhan handed him over, her eyes marred with pain. She watched as Dagda lifted the baby into the air, making him squeal. "And what about custody?" he said, glancing at the man.

"That will be decided by the courts."

Dagda's eyes narrowed. "God damn it, Siobhan. You know why you can't do this."

"I know no such thing," she said blandly, reaching for Mior. "I am a fully functioning human being, Dag."

"Not for long."

"What did you just say?" the lawyer asked, surprised.

"She heard me and she knows what I mean."

"I suggest a restraining order," the lawyer said, glancing at Siobhan. "That sounded like a threat."

"Leave us alone, Dag. We have business to discuss."

"I will not leave you alone. This is my life too and Mior is my son. You have no right to do this."

Siobhan glanced at the lawyer before turning back to him. "We have already established that I have every right to do this. Just be glad I'm not planning to list the abuses I've suffered at your hands."

"Abuses? What in hell are you talking about?"

"You hurt our daughter, Dag. You forced her to do things that were against her nature."

The lawyer's eyes widened. "Did he sexually abuse your daughter?" he whispered.

"No," Siobhan said. "But he did expect her to do illegal things. It is because of her that I decided to seek a divorce."

Dagda's mouth turned into a thin line. "When I find her, I'll…"

"You'd better not do anything," Siobhan interrupted. "If you do, you'll go to jail. I will make sure of it."

"For all the gods' sake, Siobhan. You know how I feel about you," he pleaded. "How am I supposed to function without you in my life?"

"You should have thought of that before you went after Katel. Please go. If you don't, I'll be forced to call the police."

"With what? Your phone is at home."

"I got a new one—untraceable," she said with a smile.

Dagda let out a roar, attracting the attention of several people. "You cannot do this!" he shouted.

A moment later a man approached. "Is this man bothering you?" he asked, pulling back his jacket to show his badge.

"Yes, he is," Siobhan said quietly.

"I think you should leave," the undercover detective said, pulling his jacket back further to show his gun.

Dagda glared at Siobhan with narrowed eyes before he turned on his heel and left the coffee shop. He walked down the sidewalk until he came to an alleyway and slipped into the shadows to wait. *I should have used my magic on her*, he thought, still fuming. But when she came out fifteen minutes later with Mior in her arms, he thought better of it. He wanted her intact, his creation, but also completely herself. If he did something to stop her behavior he wouldn't feel the same about her. Right now she was a fully functioning entity on her own. And he loved that about her. When she climbed into an Uber he shifted into a raven and followed at a distance.

The raven that was Dagda watched from the top of a telephone pole as Siobhan entered a low-slung apartment building, heading through a door that said office above it. The long one-story brick building located in a low rent suburb, looked to be mostly studio apartments. A few minutes later she came out and followed an East Indian man along the walkway. He stopped in front of one of the apartments and opened it, letting her go ahead. A few minutes later she was out again, the manager waiting as she held the baby in one hand and fished inside her bag, coming up with a stack of bills which she handed over. Where in hell had she gotten all that money? He'd been careful to keep her low on funds just in case something like this happened. *Only money for groceries*, he'd told her. *I will take care of everything else.* Now that she had Mior, the household funds had been increased to include what she needed to take care of him, but not enough to explain being able to slap down a deposit and first and last month's rent on an apartment. Did she have fake ID too? How long had she been planning this? Fury rose up, a harsh caw coming out of his beak before he could stop it. When Siobhan looked up, he flew away.

It was an hour later that Dagda strode down the sidewalk, his anger so palpable that people skirted wide to avoid him. He banged on number eight. It was only a second before the door opened, revealing Siobhan's pale tear-streaked face. He heard Mior crying, and pushed by her to pick up the red-faced baby, soothing him as Siobhan glared at him with her arms crossed.

"I want you home," he said in a low tone. "Mior is mine too. I've done everything in my power to keep you happy. Why are you doing this to me?"

Siobhan shook her head, tears welling. "I'm not your property, Dag. I have autonomy now. You can't just order me around and treat me like a piece of furniture you picked up at an antique auction."

Dagda sat heavily on the bed, the baby cradled in his arms. "Have I made you feel that way? If so, I'm sorry. I tried to create a beautiful life for you, for us. You know I feel about you."

"But what about your daughter, Dag? What about her inclusion in our life? You've done everything in your power to hurt her. Why?"

Dagda ran a hand across his unshaven face. "She's dangerous to me—to us. She could bring me down."

"But she hasn't, has she? As far as I can tell, she agreed to work for you in good faith. It was what you were doing that set her off. Where is she now? Have you hurt her?"

Dagda shook his head. "I don't know where she is." He let out a heavy sigh. "I'm already in the process of dismantling my life. Please don't leave me, Siobhan."

"Does that mean you'll stop your criminal activities?"

Dagda nodded, placing the sleeping baby on a pillow on the floor. "Please, Siobhan. Have a heart."

Siobhan's gaze softened as Dagda approached her. He took her in his arms, tears falling in her hair. "I need you more than you'll ever know." When he tugged at her clothing she didn't complain, allowing him to remove her sweater and unhook her bra. He bent to kiss her breasts.

Siobhan pulled away to gaze at him. "I will allow this only if you promise me that you will undo all the evil you have done, and that you reach out to our daughter to make amends."

"I promise," he murmured. "And you know when I make a promise, I keep it."

"Really?" she asked, watching him with her head cocked. "Know this, Dag. If you do not make good on this one, I *will* go through with the divorce."

He met her gaze. "I can't lose you, Siobhan. You're my reason for living."

Siobhan smiled sadly and pulled him to her. "I love you too, but there comes a limit," she whispered.

Dagda pressed her down on the bed and took his time, reveling in the smallness of her, the lemony scent of her skin. There was a fragileness to her body that aroused him, but also scared him, as though he could break her in half if he wasn't careful. He went slowly, waiting for the small sound she always made that indicated she was ready for him. He loved this part, the holding back, the waiting, knowing that once she was there, they would soar into the heights together. With Siobhan it was a spiritual coupling, their connection deep and true. "I love you," he moaned as he felt her open to him. "Oh gods, how I love you."

The baby woke them sometime later and Siobhan threw on a robe and went to feed him, retrieving the jars of baby food from the kitchen. Dagda watched her as he rose to dress. "Once you're finished with that we should get a move on," he said, pulling on his trousers.

Siobhan looked up from where she sat on the floor spooning food into Mior's mouth. "I'm not coming home, Dag. I paid for this apartment and I plan to stay here, at least until you can locate our daughter and prove to me that you're keeping your promises."

Dagda let out a snort of anger. "I have no idea where she is, Siobhan. Are you telling me you plan to live here by yourself?"

"That's exactly what I'm saying. I'm planning to take some classes at the community college and make some friends."

Dagda stared at her. "What? Since when do you care about any of that?"

"Since my daughter alerted me to the fact that you were controlling every aspect of my life. It's time I become a fully functional human being."

"You are fully functional—what are you talking about?"

Siobhan turned back to the baby. "I'm tired of being secluded and having no friends."

"Goddamn it, Siobhan!" Dagda roared. "If I had known…"

"If you'd known what, Dag—that bringing me back from the dead would turn me into a real person who doesn't always agree with you?"

"That's not fair. You know how I feel about you—I want you with me."

Siobhan rose and leaned down to pick up the baby. "If you want to see me you'll have to call and make a date. I need some time to myself before I decide what I want to do."

"What if I find our daughter and get her to live at the house?"

"If you manage that, please let me know," she said, carrying the baby into the bathroom. The water turned on, her voice whispering sweet words to Mior as she prepared his bath.

Dagda threw the bathroom door open where it banged loudly against the wall. "What in hell has gotten into you?" he demanded.

Siobhan shrugged from where she kneeled next to the tub, the baby splashing water and gurgling.

"I asked you a question, Siobhan, and I expect an answer," Dagda continued in a low tone.

She turned to look at him. "Am I not behaving as you

would wish me to?" she asked sweetly.

He let out an annoyed sigh. "I'm leaving, but I plan to be back here tonight. Don't go anywhere."

"I may or may not be here, Dag. I haven't made my plans yet."

Dagda glared at her, his face turning red. "You'd better be here. You're my wife."

"Wives are not property," she said, turning back to scrub Mior's back with a sponge.

"Why did you just make love to me if you feel this way?"

"What does that have to do with it? I enjoyed what we did together."

"Forget it," he said, backing away. "I'll see you tonight."

"Don't count on it!" she called out.

Dagda left the apartment fuming, his mind swirling in confusion. He couldn't understand her behavior or her attitude. She'd never been like this, not even the first time around. She'd turned into a different person, one that he wasn't sure he liked. As far as her ultimatums, how in hell was he supposed to find Kat and bring her home? He kicked at a rock, sending it spinning away. This was all Kat's doing. If she hadn't filled Siobhan's head with these asinine ideas they'd still be happily ensconced in their mansion.

He'd lied when he told her he was dismantling his businesses. He had no intention of doing any such thing. Tweaking things and burying them a bit deeper was all he had to do. As far as Siobhan, if she forced him to work his magic on her, then so be it. He needed her by his side, not wrapped up in a life of her own. Striding down the sidewalk lost in his thoughts, he barely noticed the blond-haired man who passed him heading the other way.

31

at found several types of greens growing in the swiftly flowing stream, her insides roiling as she stuffed her mouth full of watercress and other plants she didn't know the name of. She was so hungry she didn't care what they were, only happy to have something in her stomach to accompany the copious amounts of water she'd drunk. By the time she crawled back to where the dragon waited, she'd decided that Nidhogg was trustworthy, her fears gone as she confronted him again. "I feel so much better," she said, squinting up at his yellow serpent eye.

"I am glad for that. I thought you might be my dinner instead of my liberator. Hel seems to be behind schedule, either that or you have distracted me from the timetable I hold inside my head."

"She provides you with your...um...cadavers?"

"Without her I would have died centuries ago. Now tell me, how will you go about finding a rage strong enough to conjure an earthquake?"

Kat paused and thought. She was furious with her father, as well as angry with Airmid and Gwen. She was pretty sure she had enough rage to cause an earthquake as well as a tsunami. "Just thinking about Dagda will be enough," she muttered.

"Dagda—what is he to you?"

"He's my father. Didn't Bran tell you?"

"He did not mention it, but I am getting the sense that there is more to this story."

"A lot more. Maybe if I tell you some of it, my rage will grow and we can escape."

The dragon let out a little puff of smoke. "I am all ears."

"Hmm…where to start."

"At the beginning, of course," Nidhogg prompted.

By the time Kat reached the part of the story where she learned of Dagda's criminal dealings, she was shouting, her arms flailing.

"Now?" Nidhogg asked, glancing around at the walls of his prison.

Kat stopped speaking, letting the fury build until she couldn't contain it another second. She saw the people dying, the spent needles, her father's indifferent expression. A crack sounded and then another, rocks splitting off from the sides of the pit and crashing to the ground. A fissure opened, running from one side to the other, the earth rumbling under her feet. She fell as the rock and earth under her feet began to move, the dragon letting out a frightened puff of flame before attempting to flee. Above them the bit of sky they could see widened, a chunk of rock hurtling down, and missing Nidhogg by an inch. "Dragon's breath!" he shouted, standing up on his hind legs to avoid another chunk of slate.

Kat crawled toward him as the earth swayed. "Help me onto your back!" she yelled, trying to be heard over the sound of the freight train that seemed to be running through the pit. The dragon lowered to his knees, swaying as he reached out a wing for her to grab hold of.

"Lift!" she yelled, holding tight to the leathery surface. "The hole is big enough!"

He flung her onto his back and spread his wings, one beat of them sending him up through the hole. A moment passed and then another as Kat stared down at the pit widening below them. Water poured in from all sides, the space filling. "Go," she urged as they continued to hover in place.

"I cannot move my wings."

"Yes, you can!" she screamed, watching the water burbling up. "Just remember how it felt to fly!"

Nidhodd let out a groan, his wings moving slightly before he was able to get momentum. When they lifted free of the entrance to the pit and moved forward, he let out a bellow of joy, flames shooting out of his mouth before his wings weakened and they plummeted back to earth. By now the earthquake had quieted, the pit wide open to the sky and filled to the brim with water.

They were barely ten feet from the cavernous mouth when Kat slid off.

"I forgot how cold it is," she muttered.

Nidhogg breathed out careful flames, attempting to warm her. "I will do what I can. It is all I have to repay you for what you have done for me."

"We still have to find Bran," she reminded him.

"Yes, that too," he happily agreed, his entire demeanor

changed since being released. "But I fear it may be a few days before my wings are strong enough to carry us very far."

"I will have to wait, then. But what will we eat?"

"Hel will come around. She always does."

"I can't eat dead humans."

"Ah, yes—just as I would not eat another dragon—although I would if I was hungry enough."

Kat shook her head, moving closer to his flame-filled breath. "You need to work your wings to make them stronger."

"I will do that once they have recovered from our escape."

Kat spent the night close to Nidhogg, her huddled body taking advantage of his regular warm breath as he slept next to her. In the morning he tried his wings again, lifting ten feet before dropping like a stone.

When Hel arrived, he was spreading and folding them, hoping the action would strengthen the muscles. "What have we here?" she cried, throwing the body down in front of him.

Nidhogg tucked in, bones crunching as his jaws closed around them. "Kat caused an earthquake," he mumbled with his mouth full. "Do you have anything she can eat?"

The goddess turned the good side of her face toward Kat, her eye the warm color of acorns. "There is nothing here unless you go to the salmon pond. It is where I sent Bran."

"Did he go there?"

"That is where I left him. If you like I can take you there."

"How? I can turn into a hummingbird, but I fear I

would freeze to death in that form."

"If you can bear to touch me, I will fly you to the pond."

By now Kat had decided that the goddess would be beautiful if it hadn't been for the deformity. Without hesitation she took hold of her hand. "Meet me there!" she called out to the dragon as her body lifted into the frigid air.

He raised his right front leg in response.

The salmon pond was tranquil and quiet, Kat's hopes of finding Bran fading as Hel dropped her off. "He's gone," she said softly.

"Of course he's gone. That was a long time ago."

"But where is he now?"

The goddess shrugged, her skeletal side turning toward Kat. "I have not seen him since then."

"Do you think he's still in Niflheim?"

Hel frowned. "How would I know that? Perhaps the fish will tell you—that is if you manage to catch one." She let out a cackle as she lifted into the air and disappeared.

Kat knew there was something special about the pond and the fish that swam in it. She could feel the energy here, as though something waited with baited breath, something arcane that was beyond her understanding. The water was cloudy and opaque, but as she concentrated her attention on it, it began to clear. Beneath the surface shapes raced, colors swirling by. "I don't want to kill you," she said, looking down. "But I may have to."

There was a flickering movement before a salmon appeared, its watery eye focused on her. It stayed put as she stared at it, wondering what she should do. When it moved off, she called out, "Wait! I need to eat!" The salmon paused and stayed there as she searched for a way to catch it. Finally she reached under her clothes to unhook her bra, removing it hastily to cast across the water and let it dangle. When the fish swam into one of the cups, she hauled it in, her breath catching when she almost fell into the pond. "Why did you let me catch you?" she asked the fish once it was lying on the rocks at the edge. "And more importantly, how do I cook you?" But the fish had given up its life by then, and didn't impart its wisdom.

The sky was growing darker by the minute when she realized she would have to eat the fish raw. She had no knife, no fire—no way to cut it or cook it. The idea was repulsive, but she was too hungry to complain. But when she turned to the fish, the meat was cooked, the skin crispy and blackened. Without even questioning how this came to be, she tore into the flesh with her fingers, salivating as she stuffed it into her mouth.

Satiated, she huddled against the rocks surrounding the pond. Not even the bitter cold could keep her from falling into a deep sleep.

Bran called to her, his disembodied voice everywhere and nowhere. She couldn't find him no matter how far she wandered and searched. Her fingers were blue with cold; she was sure she had frostbite. Bran plagued her dreams and her waking, something hollow in his voice signaling that he was either no longer of this world, or very close to being gone from her life forever. Frantic to find him she ran along the ice floes, the salmon whispering in her ear. 'He is here, no that's not right—he's over here,' the fish told her. And when she did what the fish asked, she grew more and more confused, dizzy with searching. Do you still love me? she asked Bran. But to that she got no answer, only a laugh that seemed to come from the salmon that watched her from its dead fish eye.

Kat woke so cold she could barely move. Her fingers were covered with a blue frost; she was unable to move her legs. It took all her concentration to bring the blood back into her limbs, the pain of moving them making her cry out. The rest of the fish lay next to her, something about the head and the eye staring at her making her gag. *I can't throw up* she thought to herself. *I need every bit of energy the fish gave me.* When would the dragon arrive? Would she freeze to death before that happened?

The dream came back in startling detail, the images of her searching for Bran, and the taunting fish, making her wonder. Bran was here somewhere—she was sure of that. As to the fish, it had offered itself up willingly, even cooking itself to keep her alive. Why would it tease her? Maybe it was a metaphor, the fish offering another way of searching for Bran that she hadn't thought of. Obviously straightforward searching was not the path to take. But if not that, then what? "Please hurry," she muttered, sending her thoughts out to Nidhogg. "I'm about to freeze to death."

Kat spent another freezing night next to the spring before she noticed the dragon's zig zag approach, his wings like a sputtering engine as he lifted and fell. He landed some distance away, his trajectory sending him skittering into a bank of ice. She hurried toward him. "Heat, I need heat," she muttering through chattering teeth.

Nidhogg turned, sending his flames dancing toward her. "Not even a hello?"

Kat crouched next to him, trying to warm her hands. "Too cold to talk."

Nidhogg snorted. "You think you have problems. My wings are so weak I could barely fly."

Kat nodded, moving closer. "I ate a salmon."

"That is good, I guess," Nidhogg responded. "Did it impart any wisdom?"

"Only that Bran is here somewhere and that if I want to find him I have to think outside the box."

"Think outside the box? What exactly does that mean?"

"It means to think about things in a new way...not just follow the same ol' same ol'."

"You speak in riddles. I expected to search with you on my back."

"I'm still working out what I'm supposed to do," Kat whispered, her arms tight around her middle.

Nidhogg moved so that his breath warmed Kat without burning her. "In the meantime, I will exercise my wings and grow stronger."

With Nidhogg there to melt ice and keep her warm, Kat's mood improved. A plan to find Bran began to form, hazy and indistinct, but definitely in the back of her mind.

It was two days before Nidhogg felt strong enough to search for Bran. While she waited Kat ate the rest of the fish, which worked on her dreams, bringing her more insights into Bran's whereabouts. He seemed very far away in a place she wasn't sure she could reach. "I think he's under the ice," she finally told Nidhogg.

"Under the ice? How could that be? I have no way of reaching an underground dwelling."

"It isn't a dwelling. He's trapped."

If a dragon could look bemused that was his expression.

"Trapped. Under the ice. And he is alive?"

Kat had a moment of fear. "I think so. I think I would know if he was dead."

"Perhaps we will need the assistance of Hel. I can fly now, but I will never willingly go into another pit."

"I don't blame you. Can you call to Hel?"

"She will come today to bring me a new corpse."

Kat suppressed her disgust. "How do you know?"

"I am aware of the time lapse between her visits."

Kat let out a sigh. She'd hoped to get started early.

Hel arrived around midday, a fresh corpse slung under her arm. She threw it down and was about to depart when Kat grabbed hold of her sleeve. "We need you," she implored.

"What now? I have fed you both."

"You didn't feed me, I…oh never mind. I have the sense that Bran is somewhere unreachable."

"And what am I supposed to do about that?" she said, turning her bad side to Kat as though on purpose.

Instead of turning away Kat made herself really look at the sinews and muscles. "I thought you could help us. You know this land and what lies beneath the surface."

Hel stilled, her good eye staring off into space. "We did have an avalanche a moon or so back. Perhaps he got trapped."

Kat's heart lurched. "If he was caught in an avalanche a month ago, he has to be dead by now."

"Bran is a god. Have you forgotten that? He does have powers, although the last time I saw him he seemed unable or reluctant to use them."

"What about the underground river—the one that no longer runs?" Nidhogg asked.

Hel turned to the dragon. "I suppose he could be lost in that tube that runs for miles and miles. But how we are to locate him is beyond my ken."

"Maybe my love will act like a homing beacon," Kat whispered, looking down at her booted feet.

Nidhogg snorted and Hel let out a bellow of laughter. "Love?" Hel said derisively.

"Yes, love," Kat repeated, fury building inside her. "I am a goddess too, if you didn't realize it. And Bran and I used to love each other. Love is just as powerful as anger, which I feel right now toward the two of you."

Hel and Nidhogg stared at her, neither one seeming in the least perturbed.

"I'm serious," Kat continued. "I've been dreaming about him."

"And do the dreams tell you where he is?"

"Well, no, but maybe with your help…"

"I know the approximate location of the former underground river, but it stretches from one side of this realm to the other. It could take many days to find him."

Kat moved away from the dragon, trying not to breath in the stench of death. He'd finished with his meal, the bloody remains strewn across the ice. "If we flew slowly, I'm sure I could feel him if he was close. Also, I can move really fast—it's one of my powers."

Hel scoffed. "Not sure how that would help. The river runs deep under the ice. Even if you knew he was close we would need to tunnel."

Kat glanced at Nidhogg's talons. "Nidhogg can dig."

"First we have to find him," Nidhogg reminded her. "And if we do not go soon, night will be upon us."

32

When Dagda arrived at the apartment his knock was met by a young brown-haired girl. "Who in hell are you? Where's my wife!" he bellowed.

The girl back away frightened, her wide eyes darting to the baby behind her. "I'm the babysitter," she muttered.

"Well I'm the father!" he roared, pushing the door open to storm by her. "Where did my wife go?" he asked, picking up the baby.

"She…she didn't say."

"Was she alone?"

"No…she was with a man. I think they were going to dinner. She said she'd be back early."

"Goddamn that woman," Dagda fumed. "Tell her I have our son," he said, heading for the door.

"But…"

Dagda ignored her, hurrying to the waiting car and driver with Mior in his arms.

By the time he reached his house Dagda realized the folly of what he'd done. He had no food for the child, and had no idea how to deal with his crying or even how to cope with his soiled diaper. "Damn it," he muttered, removing the baby's diaper and putting him into a tub of water to clean him off. Once he was clean, he wrapped him in a towel and carried him downstairs to the kitchen, placing him in his high chair while he searched for the box of pabulum he remembered seeing months before.

He fed the baby pabulum mixed with cream, trying to let go of his rising panic. This was not the right food. He could tell by how the child spit it out and scrunched up his face. "I'm sorry, Mior. I'm new at this," he muttered. The baby had eaten barely any of the concoction when Dagda decided to call it quits. He let Mior wander naked while he used his cell phone to call his secretary. "I need live in care for Mior," he told Beatrice.

"I'll see what I can do," the older woman answered.

"That isn't sufficient, Beatrice. I need someone here now—I mean tonight."

"But sir, there is no one I can…"

"If you don't find someone, you're fired."

He hung up and paced, watching the baby crawling around the living room. A second later a lamp toppled, crashing to the floor, the cord still wrapped in Mior's hands. "Odin's ghost!" Dagda roared, rushing to untangle him.

It was sometime around ten when the doorbell rang, a petite and attractive woman in her twenties standing there. "I'm Kathy. Beatrice called me, she said…"

"Come in. I have baby duty and I don't know what I'm doing. He's upstairs asleep, but he isn't wearing a diaper. Can you rectify that?"

"Of course, sir. Where did you say he is?"

"Follow me."

The bedroom reeked of feces, the baby awake and crying, his crib a mess of excrement. Kathy's green eyes went wide, her nose wrinkling in horror. Dagda went to Mior and picked him out of the stinking crib, carrying him to the bathroom for another bath.

"What do you want me to do?" the woman asked, peering into the bathroom.

"I want you to clean up the mess. The washer and dryer are downstairs. And once you've done that please come and get the baby, dress him and put him back to bed. I have to get some rest."

"Yes, sir," she said, glancing at the baby before turning back to the bedroom.

It was nearly midnight before Mior had been dressed, fed and quieted, the crib covered in new sheets. Dagda had watched in silence as Kathy soothed Mior and found the jars of baby food in the cupboard, feeding him expertly before carrying him upstairs to bed for the second time.

"Where do you want me to sleep?" she asked, once Mior was asleep.

Dagda pointed down the hall. "Room at the end is made up. How long can you stay?"

"I can stay a week, but if you need me longer than that, I'll have to make arrangements."

Dagda nodded. "Seems like you have a handle on things. I'll be gone when you get up in the morning."

"Yes, sir. I'll be all right."

"My cell phone number is on the refrigerator if you have any problems."

Dagda had just fallen asleep when he heard shouting, someone banging on the front door. He hurried past Kathy in the hall, rushing down the steps to open the door. Siobhan was livid, her face red and swollen with crying. "How dare you!" she shouted.

"Keep your voice down. I hired a woman to live in."

"You utter bastard! You think you can just take Mior and keep him here?"

"I did, didn't I?"

Siobhan glared at him. "I thought you'd changed your ways, but it seems I was wrong. I'm filing for a divorce, Dag, and I'm positive I will be awarded full custody when I tell them what a complete bastard you are."

Dagda grabbed her shoulder and tugged her into the living room. "You will do no such thing, Siobhan." He waved his hands in front of her face, and when her eyes glazed over, he moved them in intricate patterns until her body went limp. He caught her up in his arms and carried her up the stairs to his bedroom, his gaze meeting Kathy's as he hurried by her in the hall.

"I'm sorry I had to do this," he whispered to Siobhan as he undressed her.

He placed her naked between the sheets and climbed in beside her. *When she wakes up in the morning it will be like none of this every happened,* he thought to himself. *She'll love me again and all will be as it was.* When a niggle of doubt went through his mind, he pushed it away, his arms encircling the woman who lay unconscious beside him. He pulled her close and drifted off to sleep.

Dagda woke in the morning to Siobhan staring down at him.

"Where are we, Dag? What is this place? Where is Katel?"

He turned over and sat up, wondering if he'd gone too far in his desire to bring her under his control. "This is where we live, Siobhan. This is our house. Katel isn't here. She has her own life."

Siobhan frowned. "She's a baby, how can she have her own life?"

When Mior let out a wail Siobhan smiled, reaching for the robe still hanging on the bed post. "You are such a kidder, Dag," she said, pulling the robe closed and heading for the door.

Dagda jumped out of bed and hurried after her, afraid of what might happen next. Kathy was coming down the hall when he emerged from the bedroom, the woman quickly averting her eyes from the sight of his nakedness. Instead of heading back to find his robe he moved past her to Mior's bedroom, peering in to see Siobhan standing there, her face of mask of confusion.

She turned when she heard him. "Whose baby is this?"

Dagda stilled, his heart speeding up as he tried to come up with an answer. "He's ours, Siobhan. You've had amnesia."

"Amnesia? What happened to me?"

"Car accident," Dagda blurted. "Mior is our baby. He's coming up on a year now."

211

Siobhan's confusion increased, her wide-open eyes moving to the woman now standing in the doorway behind Dagda. "Who are you?"

"I'm Kathy. Your husband—he is your husband, isn't he? He hired me to take care of Mior."

Siobhan stared at Dagda who hadn't moved. "Why…how long have I been…?"

"Come, sweetheart, let's take this one step at a time," Dagda said, stepping forward to take her arm. "Kathy will deal with Mior while you and I have a nice little chat."

He led Siobhan by Kathy, his eyes meeting the young woman's troubled gaze before she hurried in to take care of the now crying baby. Siobhan seemed stunned, not complaining as he tugged her toward their bedroom. Once she was inside with the door closed, he said, "I'm sorry this had to happen. You've been in the hospital for a while. The docs thought you were okay to go home, but it seems they were wrong."

"Hold me, Dag," she said, trembling.

My poor sweet girl," he murmured, pushing her hair aside to kiss her neck.

She clung to him as he removed her robe and helped her into bed. When his lips touched hers, her mouth opened and she pressed close as though the familiarity of him could make up for all that she was missing. Dagda tried not to think about it as he made love to her, his eyes welling as the enormity of what he'd done washed over him.

When he left the bedroom, Kathy was carrying Mior downstairs, her long hair loose around her shoulders. She stopped when she saw him, a look of sympathy crossing her features. "I heard shouting. Is your wife all right in the head?"

"No. She has amnesia. She doesn't even remember our baby." He reached out to run his hand over Mior's head. "I'm devastated."

"Of course, you are," Kathy said, concern in her eyes. "If you need anything, please don't hesitate to ask."

"Thank you, Kathy. I appreciate that," he said with as much sincerity as he could summon.

33

Bran struggled down the ice tunnel, his thoughts on Kat. It was though she was here with him, trapped under the ice and walking next to him. He felt her close by, her love sustaining him as he tried to find a way out. When the avalanche struck, he'd been carried a long way, the torrent of ice forcing his body into a deep crevasse that filled up over his head. He'd been unconscious for a long while, waking to the knowledge that he could never dig himself out. His body was covered in cuts and bruises, and a headache that felt like his skull was splitting in two kept him still for a long time after that. When the headache finally dulled enough for him to take a look around, he realized he was in a tunnel carved out of ice, maybe from some river that had flowed here in the distant past. He pushed up to his knees and crawled until the tunnel widened enough for him to stand. Along the way he found ancient dead creatures trapped in the ice which he pried out with his knife and swallowed whole. He didn't know what they were, nor did he care as long as they kept him going.

His earlier wish to die had been replaced with a fierce

desire to see Kat again, as though she'd visited him during his unconscious state. But as time passed and he grew weaker, his ability to keep going diminished. He remembered Hel telling him that he was a god and could not die, but he didn't believe her—he'd witnessed the end of several gods. They were vulnerable, not like humans, but in other ways. If it wasn't for the image of Kat he held inviolate in his mind, he would have given up long ago.

He could see in the dark, but even so he had no idea how long he'd been in the ice tunnel. It kept going and going, meandering up and down with no openings to the surface. It had no end. He would die here and never be found.

The despair increased and took him over. His body was so cold that he couldn't feel his fingers or his toes. Kat was there again, egging him on, telling him she was close by and not to give up. But he knew she was like a mirage in the desert—a figment of his imagination.

He'd come full circle now, at first deciding he didn't love her, had probably never loved her, until he knew he was kidding himself—that her presence in his life had been a blessing. She was his soul mate, a goddess as he was a god. They could have had a life together. But now it was too late, he'd disappeared off earth and she would never find him; she'd probably never heard of the Norse worlds or this godforsaken ice realm of Niflheim. And even if she had, how would she know he was there? He cried then, the tears freezing on his cheeks. His heart slowed, his sight dimming as he slid down to sit with his back against the curve of the tunnel. The cold took him, icy fingers wrapping around his body to enclose him in a false warmth. He closed his eyes and gave himself over to death.

In his dream he thought he heard Kat's voice, the sound of a conversation going on somewhere close. A scraping and scrabbling came to his ears; someone digging. *They have finally come for me*, his inner voice said. *Death is here and ready to carry me away. I wonder what death is like…* Blinding light, a scream and then sudden blackness.

34

"Pull him out!" Kat shouted, staring at the frozen emaciated man who lay crumpled in front of her.

"How am I supposed to do that?" Nidhogg asked.

Kat was on her knees next to Bran, trying to feel for a heartbeat. "He's dead!" she screamed, tears pouring down her face.

Hel reached for Bran, her enormous arms going around him. "I thought he was dead once before. Let us hope you are wrong." She pushed herself up and out of the hole they'd dug, taking Bran with her.

Kat was crying so hard she hardly felt the wing that came around her, hoisting her onto the dragon's back. "Hold on," he ordered as his wings began to move up and down. The dragon lifted, taking Kat up and out.

When they reached the top Hel was bending over the limp body laid out on the ice. "He is alive, but barely. The best I can offer is for you to take him to Frigg. She is a healer."

"How? He's unconscious."

"Nidhogg can transport you to where the realms

intersect. From there you will have to get him to Asgard, the realm of the gods."

"If he is still unconscious, I will risk carrying him to Odin's castle," Nidhogg said. "But I will have to leave you far from the front door."

Kat felt a moment of panic, her gaze on the gaunt and haggard face. He had a filthy beard that was filled with ice shards, his hair tangled and past his shoulders. He was not the man she remembered, but at least he was alive. For now.

The trip to Asgard was a terrible ordeal, Kat struggling to keep herself and the man she held in her arms from sliding off. He had not made a sound and his heartbeat was so faint she could barely hear it.

"He needs warmth and food," Nidhogg said when they arrived at the intersection, "and since he is no better now than we left, I will carry you into Asgard. I only hope that Odin does not spy me there."

"Thank you," Kat murmured, salt tears landing on Bran's face.

Nidhogg came down in a meadow, the castle looming in the distance. He took a look around before saying, "Perhaps I can fly you a bit closer. You will never make it from here."

The next time he landed they were just outside the castle walls. "I must leave you here," Nidhogg said, moving to his knees to allow her to slide off.

Kat tried to hold onto Bran as she slid off, but he was too heavy for her and landed on his back on the ground. He made no sign that he'd felt anything. "Thank you, Nidhogg. I'm glad you're free now."

"For what *that* is worth," the dragon quipped, rising into the air. "Good luck," he called as he flew away.

Kat left Bran where he was and hurried to the gate standing open. She rushed through it and ran toward the heavily carved entrance. When the door opened in response to her banging, a gaunt older man peered out, one rheumy eye widening, the other covered with a patch. "And who might you be?"

"I'm Katel, Dagda's daughter? I have Bran the blessed with me," she said, pointing toward the gate. "He's unconscious."

"I knew that young god was going to get himself into trouble. What has happened?"

"It's a long story. Can Frigg help him?"

Odin looked bemused for a second. "I will get her," he said, turning.

"And a stretcher to carry him!" Kat called out.

Instead of a stretcher, Odin accompanied Frigg and Kat to where she'd left Bran. The old god lifted him like he weighed nothing and went ahead as Frigg questioned Kat about his condition.

"All I know is that he's unconscious. We found him frozen in an underground tunnel."

"Are you saying you were in Niflheim?"

Kat nodded. "He led me there to find him."

Frigg smiled. "You are the one he spoke about the last time he was here. He seemed to be on some sort of quest, but he never revealed what was going on other than his fury with your father."

Kat let out a long sigh, unable to offer any insight.

It was two days before Kat got word that Bran was awake. She'd been given a room and told to be patient, her meals brought to her by one of the handmaidens that waited on Odin and Frigg. She was staring out the window into the garden when she heard the knock, whirling around when the door opened to emit the young woman named Sele. "Frigg asked me to take you to the sick room," Sele said, smiling.

"He's alive," Kat murmured, hurrying after the slender woman wearing a nondescript purple gown.

When she entered the room, the first thing she saw was Bran's clean-shaven face, his formerly filthy hair washed and pulled back and tied with leather. He turned when he heard her, his thin face transforming into a smile.

She rushed toward the bed, her hand reaching for his. "Bran, oh my god."

"Oh my god, indeed," he whispered. He pulled her close and buried his face in her hair.

He sobbed quietly while she tried to control her own tears, finally giving up and letting them fall. When their eyes met she noted the sadness in his, the desolation that still lingered. "What happened to you?" she asked, sitting next to him.

He shook his head and stared down at his hands. "After the Brant thing I felt like I was losing my mind...with your memories gone I couldn't tell you what was going on. Gwen made me promise not to reveal my true identity. She said you wouldn't be able to handle it. It was like living inside a nightmare. I had to break free, Kat. I had to reclaim who I am. But once I left you, it was worse. I figured out that without you I'm nothing—nobody. So I..."

She reached for his hand. "You wanted to die."

Bran nodded, his eyes welling. "I was on my way when you found me. Frigg said I was hanging on by a thread."

"And still will be if you don't take care," Frigg added, coming into the room. "Bran has a lot of healing to do, both physically and emotionally," she told Kat. "But with you here I'm sure it will go much faster."

"But he's a god—aren't gods supposed to…?"

"It is true that gods and goddesses can withstand great pressures, but when it comes to affairs of the heart, all bets are off."

Kat stilled, her gaze going from Frigg to the man on the bed. "Is this my fault—did I do it?"

Frigg shook her head. "No, Kat. Bran is a free agent despite how you two feel about each other. It was his choice to put himself in peril."

Once Frigg fussed over him and plied him with her latest tea concoction, she left them alone, telling them not to be physical for the time being.

"Does she really think I'm strong enough for that?" Bran asked.

"Where there's a will there's a way," Kat said, waggling her eyebrows.

Bran laughed before collapsing back against the pillows. When he paled Kat put her hand on his brow. "You need to rest. I'll be back later."

"You won't leave me, will you?"

"Are you kidding? I just spent a horrible endless time searching for you and nearly died in the process. I love you, Bran."

"I love you too. I feel like I'm having a wonderful dream

that's about to end."

She smiled. "This isn't a dream."

It was another week before Bran was up and walking in the garden. A steady diet of bone broth and good food had brought the color back into his gaunt cheeks, his eyes losing some of their dullness. Kat brought him up to speed on what had happened, regaling him with stories of Dagda and his exploits and her reactions to him. "He can be so great and then turn into a monster a second later."

Bran nodded, leaning on her. "That sounds like him."

"First thing I have to do when we get back is talk to Mom," Kat continued. "She was furious when I told her what Dad was up to with his businesses. For all I know she might have left him."

"He's something else, your father. I can't believe his pursuers haven't found him by now."

"He may have had them killed or paid them off. He'll do anything to stay on earth. He hates me, Bran. He blames everything on me."

Bran's eyes narrowed. "I wish I was feeling stronger. I'd like to drag him back to Otherworld to stand trial. Either that or strangle him."

"You'll get your chance. He's going down."

Bran scoffed. "Are you planning to do it?"

Kat stopped by a gooseberry bush, plucking a few off and popping them in her mouth. "Between the two of us and his enemies I'm sure we can manage something." She handed Bran a gooseberry.

Another week passed by before Frigg declared Bran well enough to leave. "Please take care of each other," she said at the door. "There is a lot of evil out there."

"And my father is the cause of much of it," Kat said, her gaze meeting Frigg's.

Frigg looked down, her cheeks reddening. "He has a few redeeming qualities, but I understand your feelings. He needs to pay the piper I suppose."

"Yes, he does," Kat said strongly. "Haven't you noticed the encroaching gray? It's his doing—the Dubh are here because of him!"

Frigg blanched. "I...I have not seen the Dubh nor have I felt them."

"I'm sorry for being so strident. I appreciate all you've done. It's just that now we have to leave the peace of your castle and Asgard and face reality. My father's actions brought the Dubh here and it is up to me to stop him."

"It is not up to you to solve all problems, Kat," Frigg said, reaching to give her a hug. "Talk to your father. He does have some good in him. Perhaps he will do the right thing."

Once they left the confines of the castle grounds, Bran turned to her. "I can turn into a raven, but that doesn't help the two of us. Not sure how to get us from here to earth."

Kat smiled. "I have a surprise for you."

35

Dagda was about to initiate relations with Siobhan when he heard the doorbell ring. "Who in hell could that be at this hour?" he grumbled, looking at the clock that showed six a.m.

Siobhan stared up at him, her expression blank. "Maybe the woman I met last night will answer it?"

Dagda shook his head and pulled on a pair of trousers, hurrying from the room. Kathy was up and heading down the stairs when he rushed by her. "Don't worry about this, Kathy—take care of Mior." He could already hear the baby cooing and gurgling. Perhaps Kathy hadn't heard him yet.

When he opened the front door, the light-haired man from the café was standing there, a file folder in his hands. "Is Siobhan here?"

When Dagda attempted to close the door, he pushed past him, his darting gaze going from one room to the other. "Your wife enlisted my help. She was adamant about wanting to get a divorce. Last night when we got back from dinner her baby was missing. She told me she was coming here to retrieve him. You have no parental rights until a court of law decides what your role should be. I've already filed the papers she signed. Where is she?"

Dagda scoffed, glancing over his shoulder at Siobhan heading down the stairs. "I suggest you ask her how she feels about it this morning," he said, gesturing.

The man hurried toward the stairs. "Siobhan? Did you find Mior?"

Siobhan stilled on her way down, her eyes going wide. "Who are you?"

"I'm Brody, don't you remember me? What happened to her?" Brody asked, turning to Dagda.

Dagda smiled. "She had a change of heart."

"The hell she did. At dinner last night she told me she was through with you. She said she wanted a life of her own, a job. She's already enrolled in the community college and has daycare lined up for Mior."

"Tell the man how you feel this morning, Siobhan."

Siobhan looked like a deer caught in headlights, her gaze going from Dagda to Brody. "I…I have amnesia. I don't remember you or anything about what you just said. I'm sorry." With that she turned and hurried back up the stairs, disappearing from sight.

Brody stared after her frowning. "She told me all about the power you have over her. She said you're a magician and can work magic. Did you hypnotize her?"

Dagda smiled. "Something like that. Run along, Brody."

Brody strode to the open door. "You haven't seen the last of me. I'm filing a police report."

"Good luck with that," Dagda said, slamming the door in his face.

When Dagda reached the bedroom Siobhan was crying, her face contorted and swollen. "Stop crying," he said, sitting next to her. "I want you beautiful for me—can you do that, sweetheart? I'll make love to you if you smile."

Siobhan shook her head and hurried into the bathroom, the click of the lock reverberating in the silence.

Dagda slammed his fist down on the bed, emotions he couldn't name rushing through him. He'd fucked it all up again. He didn't want her this way, he wanted the free and independent woman she'd become. And yet that woman didn't want him. "Goddamn it!" he roared, picking up his shirt from where he'd thrown it the night before. He put it on and tucked it into his trousers, not even caring that the linen was badly wrinkled. He stared unseeing out the window, all too aware of the sobs coming from behind the bathroom door. "I'm heading to work now, Siobhan. I'll see you later," he called as he left the bedroom.

At his office Dagda fumed and paced. Everything was upside down now, his life a disaster he didn't know how to restore. This was Kat's fault from the get go. If it hadn't been for her meddling Siobhan would be as she had been, her own person who loved Dag and would do nearly anything to make him happy. Now she was an automaton who he could barely abide. Making love to her was like making love to a fish, her responses non-existent. His fist shot out, tearing a hole in the wall as he let out a roar of fury. He waited for the inevitable query from Beatrice until he remembered that he'd fired her this morning when she said something that set him off. He had literally no one to count on now.

When he glanced out the window the encroaching grayness caught his eye; he had to admit he'd felt it in town. People were turning lack-luster, just like his wife, their minds as colorless as the forest in the distance. Was this his doing? Kat had said it was, but Kat was against him and had been since the day he first came into contact with her. What daughter behaved this way toward their father? He was a god and deserved to be treated as such. When Frigg came into his mind he let out a sigh of relief—someone he could count on to help him through this godawful mess he'd created. Just the thought of lying with her had already erased his bad mood. He left the office and searched for a secluded spot in which to shift into his raven form, his mind on Asgard and his beautiful Frigg.

"Get out of here!" Odin shouted, glaring at Dagda out of his one good eye.

"I need help, Odin. My wife is having problems."

The door was partially open and Dagda could see a skirted figure in the shadows. "Frigg?" he called out.

"How dare you call out to my wife after I told you to leave!" Odin yelled, attempting to close the door. "It's enough that your daughter was just here, why must we endure your rudeness?"

Dagda stuck his foot between the door and the jam, standing firm. "When was Katel here and why?"

"She brought Bran the blessed to my wife for healing."

Dagda's eyes narrowed. "And where are they now?"

"On their way back to the world where you live, I imagine."

"What is going on?" Frigg asked, coming up behind Odin.

"This bastard will not leave the premises."

Frigg peered out the partially closed door. "What do you want, Dagda?"

"I need to speak with you regarding Siobhan. It's serious."

Frigg pushed Odin gently out of the way. "I must be of service when I'm called, Odin," she said in a soothing tone. "I know your hatred for this god, but his wife is my patient."

Odin shook his head and backed away.

"Come in," Frigg invited, a scowl on her features. Once Dagda was inside the castle, she closed the door and turned to him. "What is it now?"

"I...I've done something that I regret and I'm not sure how to undo it." He glanced down the hall where Odin's shadow lingered. "Can we speak privately?"

Frigg's gaze narrowed. "I will not lie with you, Dagda. If you have a problem to discuss regarding the health of your wife, I am willing to listen, but anything more than that is out of bounds."

"Why?" he whispered.

"I do not have to give you a reason. Now please tell me the nature of your problem."

Dagda looked around the echoing hall. "Here?"

"Yes. I do not want you cajoling me into doing something I will regret."

Dagda grinned. "So, you do want me."

Frigg shook her head and took hold of his arm, whisking them into her tower room. She turned to him with her hands on her hips, waiting.

"Frigg, I need you," he muttered, reaching for her.

She slapped his hands away. "No sex, Dagda. What has happened to Siobhan?"

Dagda sat on the bed and rubbed a hand over his face. "I had to take a few of her memories, and now she's…"

"Didn't you learn anything the last time? What have you done to her?"

"She…she was leaving me, Frigg. I had to do something, didn't I? I couldn't let her get a divorce and take my baby away from me."

Frigg let out a lengthy sigh. "And?"

"She's…she doesn't remember Mior. I told her she was in a car crash and has amnesia. She's like an unresponsive automaton now."

"So, the sex is bad and she's not the woman you fell in love with. Good job, Dagda."

"Sex isn't bad, exactly, but it would be better if she enjoyed it."

Frigg's mouth dropped open. "You are a pig, Dagda. I told your daughter
you had redeeming qualities, but I'm reconsidering that assessment. You got yourself into this so get yourself out. And do not come here again." She placed her hand on his arm and a second later they were standing outside the castle walls.

"Frigg, please!" he begged, reaching for her. "I need you."

She pulled away and glared at him. "Goodbye," she said. A second later she was gone.

Dagda stood there for several minutes, trying to make sense of what had just happened. Frigg was his last hope, the one he'd relied on to bring him out of his funks.

Without her and without Siobhan, he was lost. Kat and Bran would show up eventually—he was sure of it. And when they did, they would both pay. His body transformed, dark wings spreading wide before he lifted into the air and flew away.

36

"**Y**ou are extraordinary!" Bran told Kat once they'd made it to Pasadena. "You have much more stamina than I do and you knew exactly where you were going."

"You thought hummingbirds weren't as bright or strong as ravens?" she asked, mocking him.

He grinned and did a one-shoulder shrug. "So, where to now?"

Kat looked up and down the familiar forested road. "One mile uphill. Are you able to walk?"

Bran nodded. "Still weak, but the adrenaline will get me through it."

Kat took his hand and tugged him forward. "I'm sure if Mom's there she'll feed us. If she's gone, Lily, the maid will know where she is."

"Let's just hope your father's at work. Not sure I'm up to a confrontation with him right now."

"It's the middle of the day so he should be," Kat assured him. "And if not, we can leave."

A half hour later she'd punched in the code and they were walking through the gates. After she rang the bell she turned to Bran, giving him a quick kiss on the mouth.

"Don't tease me, Kat. I can't take it right now."

"Sorry. I'm just so happy to be with you."

He nodded, giving her hand a squeeze just as the door opened, revealing an unfamiliar brown-haired woman. "Yes?" she said, looking them up and down.

"Hi. I'm Kat and this is Bran. Is my mother home?"

"Oh…um…yes, she's here. Your father didn't mention that you'd be arriving today."

"He didn't know. Can we come in?"

"Of course," she said, moving aside. "I'm Kathy. Your father hired me to take care of your baby brother."

"I thought Mom was doing that. Is she sick?"

"Not exactly," Kathy said, closing the door behind them. "If you wait in the living room, I'll tell Siobhan that you're here."

When she left the room, Kat turned to Bran. "Something's wrong. Lily isn't here, and Mior…Mom would never let someone else take care of him unless there was something seriously wrong with her."

"We're about to find out what," Bran said, nodding toward Siobhan who was carefully descending the stairs.

"Mom!" Kat called, running toward her. Siobhan stopped in mid-stride, her uncertain gaze on Kat.

"Are you…are you Katel?" she asked. "I…well…you're all grown up!"

Kat glanced at Bran before holding out her hand to help the fragile seeming woman down the last few steps. When they reached the living room Siobhan sank onto the couch. "Did your father tell you about my amnesia?"

"Amnesia? No. The last time I was here you were

furious with him. I thought you might split."

"Split—you mean leave him? He said I was in a car crash. I guess it happened since you were here. How long ago was that?"

"A month, maybe more? I've been in Niflheim trying to find Bran. You haven't met him yet."

Siobhan looked stunned as Bran came close to shake her hand. "So very nice to finally meet you, Siobhan. Kat has told me so much about you."

"I'm sorry. I have little memory of the recent past. I don't even remember my baby."

Kat frowned. "You don't remember Mior? Since when?"

"Since your father brought me home from the hospital? I don't even remember being there." She laughed shakily.

Kat turned to Bran. "He did something to her," she hissed.

Bran nodded. "What is your last memory, Siobhan?"

"I…I remember waking up in my bed a few days ago. I also remember a life with Dag and my baby girl, Katel. But that was obviously many years ago."

"Do you know who Dag is?"

Siobhan turned her gaze to Kat, a blank look on her face. "Who he is? What do you mean?"

Kat let out a sigh. "He's a god, Mom. And he's obviously messed with your memories. You must have been about to leave him or something."

Siobhan didn't say anything, her lips moving but no sound coming out. "Dag is a powerful man, I do know that," she finally said.

Kat shook her head and took hold of Bran's hand. "I think we need to go before Dagda gets home."

"You're leaving so soon? I thought perhaps we could get re-acquainted. I'm so sorry I don't remember you."

"I'll be back, Mom. But I need to check some things first."

"Of course. I'll be here. Your father tells me it will be a long while before I can venture outside this house."

Kat's anger rose, the wind rising with it, tree branches bending and limbs breaking to scatter wildly. Bran glanced out the window. "Are you doing that?" he whispered.

"I might be. Come on, let's get out of here." She gave her mom a kiss on the cheek before she and Bran hurried from the house. As soon as they exited the property and Kat took a couple of deep breaths the wind died down. "Crap, that's Dad," she said, pointing to the car cresting the hill. She grabbed Bran's hand and took off, racing into the forest. When she turned into a hummingbird, Bran shifted behind her, his dark feathers ruffling in the increasing wind.

Instead of heading somewhere familiar, Kat's hummingbird mind took them further up into the mountains, some instinct driving her on. When she shifted Bran did the same, both of them taking a look at where they'd ended up. "This is unexpected," he said, his gaze of the dense forest. "I thought we would go to the city or back to where we lived before…before all this shit went down."

"I don't know what brought me here. Maybe I needed the solace of the woods."

When she began to cry Bran put his arms around her. "We'll figure it out, Kat."

She pulled away and wiped at her tears. "How? He took her memories, the same thing he did to me. I don't know how to restore them."

"We'll come up with a plan. And from what you said you're immune to his crap now. Maybe you *can* restore them, you're just not aware of how to do it. This hummingbird thing is new, right?"

Kat nodded, snuggling close to warm up and to feel the realness of him. She still couldn't believe they were together. "This winter is lasting forever. I'm so sick of being cold."

Bran scoffed. "Niflheim is colder—just remember that. I'll make a fire," he said, letting her go to search for wood.

"I think I came up here because I want to stick around and see what goes on at the house. I have a weird feeling that this situation is more complicated than it seems."

"Yeah?" Bran answered, arriving with an armload of twigs and limbs.

"She was seriously pissed off the last time I saw her. Dad wouldn't have taken her memories without a very good reason."

"That's probably true. So, hang around and see who comes and goes?"

"Yes. Do you think you can conjure us dinner?"

Bran let out a chuckle. "I can catch us a rabbit and cook it. Is that to your ladyship's liking?"

Kat punched him in the arm before leaning in to kiss him, a kiss that lasted for an eternity as they clung together. "Oh…I forgot," she murmured at the end of it, staring into his beautiful mossy eyes.

"I didn't," Bran said, leaning in for another.

37

"Why is there a hummingbird flying around at this time of year?" Dagda muttered, walking toward the front door. When he entered the house, the bird hovered outside the window as though watching him. "I'm getting paranoid," he muttered, pulling the curtain across.

Siobhan lurched down the stairs, shivering as though with cold. "Katel came by today. She had a man with her named Bran. She's all grown up, Dag. I remember her as a small child. How can this be? So many years lost..." Her eyes welled.

Dagda let out a huff of anger before pulling her close. "Your recovery has taken a long time," he murmured into her hair. "I wish I'd known that Katel was coming today. I would like to talk with her."

"I'm sure she'll be back. She had some very odd things to say about you." Siobhan let out a shaky laugh.

"What did she say?"

"She told me you're a god, and that you erased my memories. She seems to think I was on the verge of leaving you and that's why you did it."

"I hope you didn't believe her. That girl is hell bent on ruining my life."

"Of course, I didn't believe her, Dag." Siobhan walked slowly over to the couch and lowered herself down. "I'm so weak and shaky. I don't know what's wrong with me."

"You've been in the hospital, that's what's wrong with you. You'll grow stronger now that you're home."

"I hope so."

When the doorbell rang Dagda went to answer it, shocked to see Brody with a detective in tow. "What in hell are you doing here again?"

"I found someone who would listen to me," Brody said. "This is Detective Emerson. I showed him the papers your wife filed and he agreed to talk to her."

"There is nothing wrong with my wife," Dagda growled. "She's been under a lot of stress and just got out of the hospital."

"Not true and I can prove it," Brody said, pulling out his phone. "I snapped off a couple of pictures while we were out together the other night." He brought up selfies of the two of them sitting at a table together. Siobhan looked radiant.

"That could have been taken years ago," Dagda said.

"Actually, it has the date on it," Detective Emerson observed, looking closer.

"And here's another with the baby," Brody continued, scrolling backward. It was taken at the apartment, and Siobhan was smiling, Mior in her arms.

"Awfully cozy with my wife," Dagda muttered.

"Well, yes. Siobhan and I enjoy each other's company. She was in the process of getting a divorce—nothing wrong with what we were doing."

"Did you sleep with her?" Dagda roared, his hands turning into fists.

Brody backed away, glancing at the detective. "We haven't reached that point yet."

"You fucker! You come here with a detective and accuse me of lying when you were luring my wife into an illicit affair?"

"Who's there, Dag?" Siobhan called, approaching the front door. She stared at Brody before glancing at Emerson. "I...told you I didn't remember you..." she began.

"Get out of here," Dagda said, waving his hands in the detective's face. "It's perfectly clear that Brody is making all this shit up. My wife has been through enough."

But instead of his eyes glazing over, Emerson's gaze went to Siobhan. "I need to interview your wife. And if you deny me this, I will get a court order. It's obvious that something has happened to her mind."

"Yes. She was in an accident."

"Your story doesn't match up with the time line Brody documented. You will either allow me to speak with her now, or I'll come back later with an order from the court. Which is it to be?"

Siobhan's hand went to Dagda's arm. "I can talk to him, Dag. I'm feeling up to it."

Dagda shook his head. "No, you will not be forced to answer questions." With that he slammed the door and threw the deadbolt across.

Siobhan stared at the door, confusion spreading across her face. "I don't understand these strange flashes I keep having. It's as though I had a dream in which that man and I were friends. How is that possible?" she asked, turning to Dagda.

"It isn't possible. I think you should go back to bed. I'll bring up dinner in a while."

"But, Dag, I…"

"You heard me, Siobhan. Go."

Siobhan headed toward the stairs, her unsteady ascent sending Dagda into a rage. This woman he'd loved and done everything for had been about to leave him for that fucker Brody! The man was nothing, not even good-looking. It was everything he could do not to race up the stairs and beat her senseless.

A flicker of movement caught his attention, his gaze going to another window where the hummingbird still hovered. *What's with you?* he mumbled, heading off to the kitchen to find something to eat. At that moment he realized that his power had not worked on the detective. He thought of the Dubh, the encroaching grayness he'd recently noticed, terror racing through him before he was able to calm himself. "I am still a god," he said to himself, dismissing his fears with a flick of his hand. He poured himself a whiskey and then another, his hand shaking around the glass.

Siobhan was staring out the window at the darkening sky when he arrived with a tray. "There's a hummingbird out there," she said, pointing. "I love hummingbirds."

When Dagda lowered the tray to the table and came to stand beside her, the hummingbird hovered for a moment and then buzzed away, disappearing into the dusky shadows. Dagda glanced at Siobhan, a wave of loathing moving through him. She was diminished, some essential part of her gone. Even her hair no longer had the luster it had, the uncertain expression on her face infuriating him. He no longer loved her, and was not even physically attracted to her. He finished the half full glass of whiskey on the tray and headed for the bedroom door. Perhaps Kathy would let him in her bed, otherwise he'd have to search out another to assuage his desires. Kat did this. It was her fault he was saddled with a weak and timid woman. "Eat your dinner," he ordered before he left the room.

Kathy opened her door wearing a nightgown, a look of surprise on her face. "What is it, sir?"

"I need a woman," he said, staring at her body under the light cotton fabric.

Her cheeks reddened. "But...what about your wife?"

"She doesn't want me. I can't go on like this. Please, Kathy."

Kathy hesitated, a frown replacing her surprise. "You've been drinking..."

"So what? I want to have sex. That's all. No strings attached. I'm a good lover and I won't hurt you." He reached to touch her face, his fingers caressing her cheek.

Kathy stared at him for a full minute before she opened her door to let him inside. "I suppose I can help with that," she murmured.

Dagda was leaving Kathy's room when he saw Siobhan watching him from down the hall. Before he could say a word, she'd turned and headed back to their bedroom, the door closing behind her. When he reached it, the door was locked. "Siobhan, open this door!" he shouted.

"Go away."

"I mean it. If you don't open this door, I'll break it down!"

When the lock clicked, he burst inside, glaring at Siobhan who glared back. "Are you screwing the help now?" she asked.

There was gumption there, a hint of the Siobhan he once knew and loved. He strode to where she stood, picked her up and carried her to the bed.

Dagda woke with a sick feeling deep inside. He'd drunk too much, screwed Kathy and then screwed his wife, his ability to hold himself back lost in the heat of the moment. "Siobhan," he whispered, moving her tangled hair aside to kiss her neck.

Her eyes opened, a frightened look in them before she pulled away. "Don't touch me," she said, rising from the bed. A second later she was in the bathroom with the door locked.

Was everything going to hell? Dagda rose and dressed, wondering how he would fix this latest debacle. He had little memory of the night before, wondering what in hell he'd done to upset her. "Siobhan," he called, knocking on the door. "I love you."

"What you did to me last night was not an act of love, Dag. When I asked you to stop, you ignored me."

"I…I don't remember you asking me to stop."

"Really? I was yelling at the top of my lungs."

Dagda stilled, his mind whirling. Had he really been that out of control? Things were worse than he realized. As a god the alcohol shouldn't have had any effect on him—or at least not much. How had he ended up so drunk that he basically raped his wife? "I…I'm sorry, Siobhan. Can you forgive me?"

"I'm not sure yet."

Dagda backed away, afraid of what he might have done to Kathy, but when he left the bedroom, she was walking down the stairs with the baby, a smile on her face when she saw him.

"Good morning, Kathy," he said hesitantly.

"Good morning, sir."

He took the toddler out of her arms, allowing her to go ahead of him. When they reached the kitchen, he deposited Mior into his high chair before turning to Kathy. "Sorry about being drunk last night," he said, fishing for details.

"Oh, you weren't that drunk."

"Really? I thought maybe I…I didn't hurt you, did I?"

Kathy laughed. "Quite the contrary." She reached for the baby food jar and set it in a pan of water to warm it up.

Dagda stared into the distance, his inability to remember either incident making him uncomfortable. He'd never been drunk like that, not even when he downed an entire bottle of whiskey. "I…I have to go to work now. Can you keep an eye on Siobhan? She isn't well this morning."

"Of course."

When Dagda exited the house, Kat was waiting for him. "I know what you did to Mom."

His expression darkened. "I did nothing to your mother—get out of my way."

"She was planning to get a divorce—is that why you took her memories? Can you restore them?"

Dagda ran a hand over his unshaven face. His eyes were sunken with dark circles under them. "I don't know. Something's wrong."

"With you? Yes, there is. You're a selfish monster." When Dagda met her gaze, Kat noticed a hint of fear in his eyes. "But what are *you* talking about?"

"I got drunk last night. I never get drunk."

"That's hardly odd, Dad."

"No, I mean I can't get drunk. I'm a god."

"So…you're saying that you're changing? That you don't have the power you once had? Maybe it's because you've abused it."

"No, Kat. Listen. I tried my magic on a detective who came

by, and it didn't work, and last night I…I had a couple of glasses of whiskey and I can't remember the details of the evening."

Kat stared at him, surprised he was standing here confessing things to her. "Maybe you should test your powers properly. Try and do some good for a change."

"Like what?" Dagda asked, his eyebrows coming together.

"Like trying to restore Mom's memories, for one. Also, redoing the mess you made in Hong Kong."

He scoffed. "That's nothing. As to your mother, I…" His gaze went into the far distance.

"What?"

"Nothing. I have to get to work now."

"I wish I had the power to bring her memories back."

"I wish you did too."

"Really, Dad? Even if she wanted a divorce?"

"She may well want one now."

"What did you do to her?" Kat asked sharply.

He shook his head and pushed by her, heading to the car that has just pulled up. A moment later he was climbing inside the Mercedes, the car speeding away a second after that. Kat hurried to the front door and rang the bell.

"Good morning, Kat!" Kathy said, holding the door wide. There was a new brightness in her eyes, her smile wide. "Your mother is still upstairs. Your father said she isn't feeling well today."

Kat wondered why Kathy seemed so changed as she ran for the stairs and took them two at a time. When she reached her parents' bedroom door she knocked. "Mom? Are you okay?"

The door opened revealing Siobhan's wan face. "I've been better, dear. Please come in."

Siobhan never explained what had happened the night before, but Kat knew that Dagda had hurt her. Either physically or mentally or maybe both. "Do you want me to take you somewhere?"

Siobhan laughed. "I have no money, no friends and no memories, Katel. Where in heavens name would I go? I am completely dependent upon your father."

"This isn't a good situation, Mom."

"Be that as it may, I'm stuck until my amnesia lifts."

"It won't ever lift. Dad took your memories."

"Please don't start with that nonsense again. I may not love him, but he does provide for me."

"You don't love him—see? That's what I'm telling you. You were about to leave—it's why he did it."

"And what about Mior? Would I leave my child behind to be taken care of by another woman? No, Kat. I have to hope that I remember this child's birth and my time with him."

Kat let out a sigh. "You won't unless we find a way to restore your memories. Mine came back, but only because I'm half goddess."

"Half goddess?" Siobhan let out a tinkling laugh, but then she grew serious. "Half goddess," she intoned. "That rings a bell. I do remember your father leaving shortly after you were born. I was okay with it. I always knew he would go at some point. He wasn't the sort to be tied down."

"Mom, you died and he brought you back from the dead."

Her eyes went wide. "But he left me when you were a baby, and…"

"He did, but he came back after my stepfather killed you."

"This sounds like some soap opera story, Katel. I married another man and...that man killed me?"

Kat nodded. "He wanted your money. I hated him."

"I wish I could remember all that, although perhaps not my death."

"Actually, you knew he was poisoning you and you went along with it. Dad said you'd always been like that...letting fate and destiny rule your life."

"Fate and destiny." Siobhan stared into the distance. "I...remember your father, Kat. He was so handsome and sweet back then. What has happened to him?"

"I didn't know him back then so I couldn't say. I think his power has gone to his head, although I wonder...if maybe his powers are disappearing."

"Powers, what an odd word that is," Siobhan said, smiling. "I agree that he's powerful. Perhaps his businesses are giving him trouble—could that be why he's been so erratic and cruel?"

"Cruel. Was he cruel to you?"

Siobhan sighed, her shoulders slumping. "He was drunk. I have to forgive him. I think I hurt his feelings when I told him about a dream I had regarding that man, Brody."

"A dream? What happened?"

"Nothing much, I just must have dreamed that I was with him—we were friends. I liked him, and it seemed as though..."

"What?"

Siobhan shrugged and leaned back against the pillow, an empty expression on her face. Kat stared at her, willing her to remember her life, but the blank look remained.

Kat left the house a half hour later, joining Bran in the

woods where she'd left him. "I have food," she announced, pulling open the bag of bread and cheese Kathy had given her before she left.

"You didn't like my rabbit last night?"

"Not really. I prefer to eat things that don't have eyes."

"Vegan or vegetarian?"

"Probably vegetarian since I eat cheese."

"You should have told me," he muttered, kicking at the carcass.

"Starvation kept me from complaining."

Bran grabbed her arm, tugging her down to sit on a log. "We need to do something about your father. I see what you were trying to tell me about yesterday—the Dubh have claimed huge swaths of land now."

"He…he confessed to me that he's losing his powers. I'm not sure what's going on, but he's definitely growing weaker."

"And your mother?"

Kat let out a sigh. "She says she can't leave him because she's dependent on him. She told me she doesn't love him."

"Wow. Are her memories returning?"

Kat shook her head, stuffing a piece of bread and cheese into her mouth. "It's March and it's still so cold," she commented after swallowing.

"I think it's the Dubh. When they take the light, they also take the warmth."

Kat looked up, her gaze on the branches of the conifer trees above them. "Hadn't thought of that, but it makes sense. I wonder if the Dubh are affecting Dad."

"Maybe." Bran lowered himself down next to her. "All I want to do is reconnect and concentrate on us, but I can't.

This shit has to be dealt with."

Kat smiled. "Me too. First thing we need is a room with a bed. Last night was…"

"Painful?" Bran laughed.

"Yup, but not painful enough to stop me from enjoying it."

The forest sighed around them, the pines whispering. A warm breeze arrived, filled with the fresh smells of spring. Bran leaned in to kiss her.

"Do you have money?" Bran asked once they'd flown to town and turned back into their human forms.

Kat smiled, pulling out a wad of bills. "I took them from Dad's stash when I was at the house."

"You little thief!"

"Learned from the best," she said, grinning. "Let's find a room and decide our next plan of action."

Bran put his arm around her shoulders. "I know what my next plan of action is," he said, waggling his eyebrows.

"But aren't you still weak from your ordeal? Maybe we should take it easy for a few days."

Bran scoffed. "I need to make up for lost time. Didn't you say where there's a will there's a way?"

Kat laughed. "I won't be complaining," she told him. Another warm breeze wafted by, filled with the scent of flowers. Kat gazed at Bran, her heart filled with love. He stared back, his moss-colored eyes lit up from within.

39

When Daniel drove up to Dagda's building, the entire place was crawling with cops. "What the hell?" Dagda muttered.

"Apparently they've gotten wind of your illegal activities, sir," Daniel said, pulling away from the curb.

"How did that happen?"

"Could be Jones, could be Beatrice. People do not like being fired."

Dagda let out an angry huff. "They deserved to be fired. What about the rest of them? Where are they this morning?"

"Like rats, they deserted the sinking ship," Daniel said quietly.

Dagda tried to decide whether to be angry with Daniel or not, his unease at an all time high. "Do you have a suggestion for how to deal with this, Daniel?"

"I would say get yourself as far away from here as you can. If these people are here, they are surely at your house as well. The FBI doesn't take kindly to gun running and money laundering."

"Goddamn it," Dagda muttered under his breath. "That means my wife is stuck there."

"Once you find a place to hide, I'll go by and pick her up."

"Thanks, Daniel. You've been very loyal."

"I enjoy my generous paycheck, sir."

"Oh shit. Does this mean they've infiltrated my accounts?"

"Didn't you say you have money in other countries?"

Dagda fell back against the leather seat and let out a sigh of relief. "Yes. Thanks for reminding me. I'd better get on the horn and transfer some cash before I'm on the damn streets."

"Yes, sir. I have an idea of a place where you can hole up until things calm down."

"Take me there."

Dagda looked around the dismal studio apartment, his gaze going to a spiderwebs in the corner. The room was filthy and smelled of stale cigarettes. But at least if was off the beaten path in a neighborhood where no one would look for him. Daniel was on his way back to pick up his wife and son with instructions to leave them there if there was any hint of cops hanging around waiting for him.

Dagda pulled off the mildewed coverlet and sat on the bed, his head going to his hands. Something was very out of balance. Would he have to return to Otherworld to set things right? But if he did, he'd never see Siobhan or Mior again. Tonight he would try to restore her memories. If it didn't work it meant that his powers were leaving him. And if that was true, he was in serious jeopardy.

It was close to two a.m. before he heard the Mercedes pull up outside. He pushed the dirty curtain back to peer out, glad when he saw Daniel open the back door and help Siobhan and the baby out. When Siobhan stumbled up the walkway Dagda rushed to open the door, taking Mior out her arms as he sought out Daniel. "What happened?" he asked the driver.

Daniel stopped on the sidewalk. "The cops were there but I created a diversion in order to retrieve your wife and child." Daniel glanced at the door where Siobhan could be seen inside the room. "She was not at all happy about this," Daniel continued. "I had a hell of a time convincing her that she needed to come with me. And when I insisted that she bring the baby along, she nearly balked."

"And Kathy? Was she there?"

"The police were questioning her in the living room when I took your wife down the back stairs and out the servant's entrance. Luckily the baby was sleeping in his room and I was able to grab him on the way."

Dagda reached into his pocket and pulled out a wad of bills. "Thanks, Daniel. You seem to be my only friend at the moment."

Daniel took the money. "I would suggest you ditch your cell phone. I'll be by with food and a new phone in the morning."

When Dagda returned to the room Siobhan was sitting on the bed staring into space. He placed the baby in her arms and turned to pour her a glass of water. "I'm sorry about this Siobhan, but I couldn't leave you there. Did they talk to you earlier today?"

Siobhan's glazed eyes met his. "Yes, Dag. They said you were a criminal and should be behind bars. They questioned me for over an hour."

"What did you tell them?"

Siobhan shook her head. "Nothing, since I have no knowledge of what you do or even where your office is." She placed the sleeping baby on the bed and rose to take off her coat. "As far as this baby, I have no memory of him—he's a complete stranger. Do you expect me to take care of him?"

"Yes, Siobhan, I do. He's your son."

"And I'm not well, Dag. I'm not up to whatever you have in mind. I think I'd prefer being in the hospital to this," she added, looking around with distaste. "Could you have picked a worse place?"

"Daniel picked it. They'll never find us here. It's only for a few days until I figure out how to get us out of this mess."

"You should have left Mior with Kathy. She's your mistress now, isn't she? And I can tell she loves Mior."

Dagda felt his ire rise. "Stop this, Siobhan. You're the mother and I expect you to act like it."

"Am I to be a wife to you too, even though we don't love each other?"

"Why do you say that? I love you. I'm sorry if…"

"No, you don't, Dag. If you did you wouldn't have slept with Kathy."

Dagda ran his hands across his face and sat heavily on the bed. "That was just sex, Siobhan. I want you back the way you were," he mumbled.

"What did you say?"

Dagda met her gaze. "I want you to be yourself, even if it means we get a divorce."

"Be myself? What does that mean? You mean like I was before the car crash?"

Dagda grabbed her hand and tugged her down next to him. "There was no car crash and no amnesia. I took your memories because you wanted a divorce. I thought we could start over, but it didn't work out the way I hoped. You've always been my reason for living. Without you in my life I may as well be back in Otherworld locked in a dungeon."

Siobhan's mouth dropped open, her eyes widening. "So…you're saying that what Kat told me is true? How can you be a god? There's no such thing!"

"You knew it back then, Siobhan. You always suspected. Dig deep and try to recall. I remember one specific day right after Katel was born. You were lying in bed feeding the baby and I appeared out of the ether. I had some business to do back in Otherworld and I didn't take my usual precautions when I returned. You were surprised, yes, but you also said you'd known there was something otherworldly about me. Do you remember that, sweetheart?"

Siobhan stared into the distance, a frown on her face. "I…I…" She paused for several minutes before she turned to face him. "Yes, I remember now. You told me you were a god, and not just a lesser god, but the all-father god. You had to leave me behind because of your duties in the other world." Her eyes welled and spilled over. "I loved you so much back then," she whispered. "I was miserable after you left. Thank goodness for Katel. She was the only thing that got me through it."

"And I loved you," he said, his fingers tracing a tear down her cheek. "I was incredulous when you got pregnant. A baby was unheard of between a god and a human. I didn't want to leave. It was probably the single most difficult thing I've ever had to do."

"What has happened to you? Why did you change so much?"

Dagda stared at the floor. "I don't know. I wanted to make you happy, and I...I went too far, I guess."

"Being a criminal? You knew how I would feel about that. Why did you do it?"

Dagda let out a sigh. "Because I could. It was so easy, Siobhan. I was making so damn much money."

"Money isn't important."

Dagda let out a humorless laugh. "Look around you. This is how we would live without it."

She shook her head. "We had a good life back then, Dag. We didn't have money. We lived in the woods in a tent and grew vegetables."

Dagda didn't answer, trying to control his tears. "I'm going to attempt to bring your memories back, sweetheart. And if it doesn't work, I'll know."

"Know what?" she asked watching him move his hands in front of her face. "Stop doing that—it makes me dizzy."

But Dagda continued, watching her features slacken and her eyes turn opaque. When she suddenly slumped forward, he caught her in his arms and placed her gently on the bed next to Mior. Dagda moved to lie down on the other side, his eyes closing on the dingy room and his sorry life.

"Dag?"

Dagda opened his eyes to see Siobhan staring down at

him. Thin early morning light drifted through the stained and greasy curtains.

"You did it," she said. But there was no smile on her face, only sorrow in her eyes.

He grabbed her hand and twined his fingers through hers. "I love you," he whispered.

She pulled away and picked up Mior, holding him close. "My sweet baby," she crooned. "Mommy's here now."

Dagda sat up, watching her. "That makes me so happy," he murmured.

But Siobhan ignored him as she placed the baby on the floor and reached for a jar of baby food.

Dagda watched her for a moment before rising and heading for the shower. She was exactly as he feared, her love for him gone.

"What do we do now?" Siobhan asked when Dagda emerged from the bathroom a half hour later.

"We wait for Daniel. He's my spy."

"If I call Brody he'll come and get me," Siobhan said, her clear gaze meeting his. "I already paid for that apartment."

"Can I stay there? I doubt anyone will think to look in that part of town. I promise I won't bother you."

"That will never work, Dag! I was planning on getting a divorce and going to school."

"And dating Brody," Dagda said morosely.

"Maybe I was. I don't know now. I feel very strange…not myself at all. Certainly not like how I felt before you took my memories."

"Are you glad I restored them, Siobhan? I did it for you. It's probably the most unselfish act I've ever performed."

"I don't know yet. But for now, I would like to move back to my apartment. My clothes and Mior's clothes are already there and I'd just stocked the place with food." She pulled her cell phone out and hit some numbers, turning her back on Dagda who sat on the bed.

"Brody? It's Siobhan…yes, that Siobhan. Can you come and pick me up?"

She stepped outside, her voice fading as she walked to the sidewalk to look at the street name and number and recited the address.

When she came back to the room Dagda was feeding the baby, unable to stop the tears from running down his face. He swiped at them and turned away, his insides twisting with a pain he'd hoped to never feel again.

When Brody arrived twenty minutes later Siobhan was dressed, the baby in her arms. "Goodbye, Dag," she said, when the knock sounded.

Dagda looked up at her. "Is there any hope at all?"

She smiled sadly. "There's always hope."

"But for us?"

Siobhan shrugged and opened the door, exiting a moment later. Dagda rose to look out the window, watching Brody kiss her lightly on the lips before taking her arm and helping her and Mior into the car. Instead of his usual anger he felt an all-encompassing sadness, his world going dark in front of his eyes.

It wasn't long before Daniel arrived carrying a paper bag. When Dagda let him in, he placed the bag on the table and pulled various things out. "Breakfast," he said, handing Dagda a cup and opening a cardboard box. "Quiche and lattes." He glanced around. "Where's your wife and Mior?"

"Brody picked them up."

"But I thought she…was ill."

"You do know what I am, don't you Daniel? I restored her memories and she left me, just as she was in the process of doing when I took them."

Daniel didn't say anything as he sat in a chair and sipped his coffee. "Sorry to hear that," he finally said.

"Yes, well, it's kind of the end of things for me. I'm out of here as soon as I can clear up a couple of things."

"And your daughter? Where is she now?"

"Hell if I know. I saw her the other day and I haven't seen her since."

Daniel pulled a cell phone out of the bag and handed it over. "Thought you could use this," he said.

Dagda took it and placed it on the table. "Where I'm going I'll have no use for a phone."

"Where's that?"

"Home."

40

Kat sat up. "Something's happened."

Bran opened one eye. "Yeah, we're sleeping in a bed. Go back to sleep, Kat."

Kat rose and began to pace the small room they'd booked. "It's Dad and Mom and Mior. Something's changed."

Bran sighed and pushed himself up to sitting and leaned against the headboard. "Something...good or bad?"

"I don't know. I have this strange feeling in my stomach. I need to go to the house and check."

"Now? It's like the butt crack of dawn."

Kat laughed. "That's a funny saying coming from a god."

"Learned it from one of the homeless guys I used to hang out with." He rose from the bed and searched for his pants.

"You don't have to come with me."

Bran stopped in the middle of pulling on his jeans, staring at her. "Why wouldn't I come with you, Kat? If something odd is happening I think I should be there."

"Okay. I just…I don't know. This feels personal somehow."

"Are we going as birds? Because if so, I'll hang out in the tree."

Kat nodded and finished dressing, her internal radar sending her mixed up messages she couldn't decipher.

When Kat reached Dagda's house the door was wide open. Inside the place had been ripped apart, papers strewn everywhere, books pulled off shelves and general chaos. No one was there. She hurried up the stairs. When she heard a heavy step, she hurried back down, hoping to see Dagda standing there, but instead it was a heavyset man in a dark suit.

He held out a badge, his narrow-eyed gaze pinning her. "Do you know the whereabouts of the man who owns this house?"

"That man is my father, and no, I don't. I was surprised to discover him gone, as well as my mom and my baby brother."

"He's wanted by the FBI for questioning about his businesses." He held out a card. "If you hear from him please call me at this number."

Kat nodded, slipping it into her pocket. "Did your men make this mess?"

He stared at her impassively. "We needed his files."

"And did you find what you were looking for?"

"Some of it, but he's clever, your father. Do you happen to have the code for the safe?"

"No." For probably the first time ever Kat felt real

sympathy for Dagda. "I suggest you lock up when you leave so that thieves don't come in and steal all the furnishings." She left the house and walked through the open front gate, following the road uphill. A moment later Bran was walking beside her.

"You look distressed," he said, concern in his mossy eyes.

"They're all gone—Dad, Mom and Mior—even Kathy. The place is a mess and the FBI are after my father." Before she could stop herself, she was crying.

"If I didn't know better I'd say you care about him," Bran said, slipping his arm around her.

She looked up at him. "I…I don't know what I feel. But the thought of him holed up somewhere and trying to evade the law makes me feel very peculiar. Especially if he's lost his powers."

Bran scoffed. "After everything he's done it's hard for me to feel anything but gratitude that he's finally been brought down." By now they'd reached the ridge line, the forest spread out before them. "Look down there, Kat, and tell me you feel sorry for him." He pointed at the colorless haze of trees. "While you weren't looking the Dubh have made inroads."

Kat squinted into the distance, fear taking up residence in her stomach. "What do we do, Bran? I have no idea how to stop them."

"This will require the summoning of all the gods. We could be on the brink of war."

"War? They can't just be chased back with magic?"

Bran's gaze darkened. "This happened once before centuries ago. Earth was spared that time; the fact that they're here now means it's much worse this go around. The entire world could be in serious jeopardy."

"And it's all Dagda's fault?"

Bran glanced away, his fingers moving though his shoulder length hair. "Not entirely. His being on earth has created an imbalance, but there's an energy that's encouraging it. Greed, and forgetting what's truly important have allowed the Dubh to flourish. My time with the homeless was very enlightening; they called it like it is here on earth. Many of them were veterans, Kat—people who fought in wars to defend this place. Others had mental problems that kept them from being able to get or keep a job, and some were just unable to make it in a world where money was the driving force. They'd been forgotten, dropped from a system that does nothing for anyone who can't pay for it."

Kat took in a breath and let it out slowly, trying to calm her fast beating heart. The word war had sent her mind skittering forward into a bleak future that she didn't want to contemplate. She'd had dreams about this—dreams in which she and Bran were fighting some unseen forces. "But what does war mean for us—for you and me?"

Bran turned his worried gaze to hers. "It means we will be the driving force to stop them, Kat. Remember who you are."

Kat shook her head and glanced away. "I need to find my father."

Bran shifted, watching her with his dark raven eye until she did the same. He flew off and she followed, her bird mind aware that something serious was happening, even though the details were foggy.

Bran was like a homing pigeon, landing on an unfamiliar street full of derelict houses and apartments. "He's there," Bran said, pointing.

"How'd you find him?"

He shrugged. "It's a god thing."

"But I'm half goddess and I didn't know where to go."

Bran gave her a shove toward a half-painted door. "Stop talking and go find your father."

Kat glanced back at him before she hurried up the weedy path and knocked on the door.

The door opened a moment later, Dagda's blood-shot eyes staring at her in surprise. "How in hell…"

She pushed past him into the dark room. "The FBI is at the house. They tore it apart looking for your files. Where's Mom and Mior?"

"She finally left me. But I did manage to restore her memories. She's with Brody."

"You look like hell, Dad. What are you doing here?"

He sighed and shook his head. "Waiting to get up the courage to head home."

"Home…to Otherworld?"

He nodded and sat on the edge of the unmade bed. "Nothing left for me here."

"I'm here."

Dagda laughed, meeting her gaze. "And you hate me, just as your mother does. I fucked everything up, Katel."

"I'll admit that you've made a mess of things. But…well…I do know how much you love Mom. I'm sorry she's gone."

"For my sake? I deserved it."

Kat stared at the unkempt, ruined man sitting in front

of her. "You're a god, and you obviously still have powers."

"What good does that do me? Your mother is gone and I have no way to get her back."

"Maybe try and reclaim the god she fell in love with."

He shook his head. "We had a moment before she left. We talked and I thought…maybe. But after I gave her back her memories, she was ready to move on."

"Where is she? I need to talk to her."

"Don't tell her anything on my account. I could leave at any moment."

"At least wait one more day. You are obviously not in any shape to face a firing squad."

Dagda scoffed. "A firing squad would be welcome compared to what's in store for me."

Kat touched his shoulder. "Will you promise to stay until I get back?"

"Why are you suddenly being nice? I've treated you like a pariah since the day we met."

Kat gazed at him. "I don't have an answer for that. But I've seen the love between you and Mom and I know that underneath your asinine behavior there's a part of you that would do anything to keep her."

"And look how well that turned out."

Kat shook her head. "That's true, but we're past that now. It's time to be real, Dad. I know that's a difficult concept for an all-powerful god who has taken advantage of a corrupt system to further his own gains, but as I said, if you want her back, you will have to reclaim the god she fell in love with."

Dagda's bleary gaze met hers. "Do your worst."

"My worst? Is that supposed to be encouraging?"

Dagda shrugged. "I hold no hope, Kat. She's moved on, and I don't blame her."

"Do you know where she is, or do I have to rely on Bran to find her too?"

Dagda frowned and straightened. "That bastard is with you?"

"I'm in love with that bastard and I expect you to accept him. Do you have an address for her or not?"

Dagda let out a sigh. "She's on Prince Street in apartment eight."

"Think about what I said. I'll be back."

Bran held back as Kat tugged him toward the Prince Street apartment. "You need to talk to her alone. I'm too pissed with Dagda right now."

"Okay. Don't go anywhere." Kat left him on a bench and hurried up the street, her mind whirling with things to say. But as soon as the door opened, she forgot everything, her concern taken by the tear-streaked face staring out at her. "What's wrong, Mom?"

Siobhan pulled her inside and closed the door. "I don't know who I am anymore. Brody's angry with me, the baby doesn't seem to recognize me..." her voice trailed off, tears sliding down her cheeks.

Kat followed her into a tiny living room and sat next to her on a loveseat. "Where's Mior?"

"He's sleeping finally, after crying non-stop for an hour. How long was I gone, Kat?"

"You mean..."

"Yes. How long ago did your father take my memories?"

"I don't know, really. A couple of weeks?"

"And in that short time my entire life has been turned upside down." She let out a sob and covered her face with her hands.

"Dad said…"

Siobhan lifted her head. "You saw him?"

"Yes. He's a miserable mess. He's planning to go back to Otherworld, which is probably a good idea, but…"

"I don't want him to go," Siobhan blurted.

Kat frowned, staring at her. "He told me you were finished with him."

"I am…I was…I don't know what I think or feel anymore. I'm a mess too."

"Mom, he loves you. I know that. He's in trouble. The FBI are after him, and…"

"I know all that. He told me. When he restored my memories, I…I wasn't the same. I mean, I'm the same person but everything's changed. Oh my gosh. I don't know how to explain any of it."

"But do you love him?"

Siobhan turned away to wipe her eyes. "I love the man he was. But after you told me what he'd done, I…I couldn't be with him anymore. I've been trying to equate that person with who I thought he was, but I simply can't. And then Brody came along. He's in love with me."

"If you could see Dad now…"

Siobhan shook her head, wiping at her tears. "I saw that man last night. Before Dag did what he did, he made me remember things I haven't thought about since…well, since he brought me back from the dead. I felt the love I had back then, relived the terrible loss when he left me." She turned away, crying. "Kat, I can't go through that again—raising our child by myself and knowing I'll never see Dag again. I just can't. But I also know he's committed crimes, both here and in Otherworld. He has to pay for what he's done."

Kat held her mother's hands, trying to comfort her and failing miserably. "Maybe there's a way," she muttered.

Kat left fifteen minutes later, a hazy plan working inside her. When she caught up with Bran, he was coming up the street, his frowning gaze on the sidewalk in front of him.

"Well? What happened?"

"I don't know yet. But it seems she still loves him."

Bran frowned, his lips thinning. "Jesus, Kat. Seriously? After everything he's done you want to play matchmaker? The guy is a serious asshole."

"And he's also my father. Mom just admitted that she doesn't want to bring up Mior alone."

"Tell her to stick with that guy, Brody. He seems like a decent sort."

Kat felt a wave of irritation. "She isn't in love with Brody."

"Are you telling me she's in love with Dagda? That seems remote at best."

"I think she may be. I understand your feelings, but…I'm still trying to sort out mine."

"All you need to do is go back a few months and think about all the shit he's pulled. Remember Hong Kong? The stories you told me were harrowing. They made me want to kill him."

Kat let out a sigh, tugging at the end of her braid

hanging over one shoulder. "I know. I'm crazy."

Bran pulled her close. "You aren't crazy. You're just a soft touch."

When Kat reached the apartment where she'd left her father, he was no longer there. A note on the table next to the cell phone read:

Please make use of this. I love you, Katel, and I love your mother and Mior. I will miss you all more than I can say. The combination to the safe is as follows. Use it wisely.

The numbers that followed were her birth year combined with Mior's. Kat burst into tears. When she exited the apartment, Bran was waiting for her, his expression knowing.

"He's gone, isn't he?" When Kat nodded, he pulled her into his arms. "I'm sorry, Kat."

Several days went by before Kat could face her mother. She didn't want to tell her Dagda was gone. But when she finally found her nerve her mother already knew. "He came to say goodbye," she told Kat. "He…he…" Siobhan broke down sobbing.

Kat noticed Mior watching and went to pick him up, trying very hard to hold her tears at bay.

Siobhan sat down on the loveseat and patted the place next to her. "I'm devastated. This is worse than the first time. Will he come back?"

Kat sat and placed the baby on the floor, surprised when he grabbed the couch cushion and pulled himself up to standing. "He's…"

"Yes, he took his first steps today and Dag missed it. He will miss all the milestones, just as he did with you. I told him I still loved him. Why, Kat? Why did he leave me?"

"You know why. Love isn't enough when you've broken all the rules. It's commendable when you think about it. He could have taken you and Mior and disappeared who knows where, but instead he's taking his punishment."

"But he's a god and will live forever. We're human and we'll die."

Her mother was right. Kat thought about what the rest of Dagda's life might look like, the horror of it filling her with dread. When she glanced at her mom, Siobhan was crying again, the expression on her face so bleak that Kat's eyes welled in sympathy. Yes, her father was doing the right thing, but not ever seeing him again gave her a very queer feeling in the pit of her stomach. Her relationship with him was complicated and filled with ambiguity. But what her mother was going through was worse.

41

As soon as Dagda stepped foot into Otherworld he was apprehended and dragged to a secure place to await trial. He didn't care what happened, glad to be done with his life. He hoped fervently that they'd give him the death sentence, although that level of punishment was very rare here. The most he could expect was a life devoid of power, the other gods and goddesses regarding him with disdain. Could he kill himself? He wasn't sure if it was possible or not, but he knew he would try.

Otherworld had been taken over by a gray pall, the Dubh visible in every part of the land. When Morrighan came to see him, he couldn't meet her gaze.

"Glad you finally decided to give yourself up," she said, watching him with narrowed eyes. "Otherworld has suffered terribly since you let loose the Dubh. I hope you spend all eternity in Hell."

"I do too, although I'd prefer death. Will you kill me, Morrighan? You have a knife sharp enough, don't you? I have hurt you as I have hurt many others. Wouldn't it feel good to be the one to take the breath from my body?"

"Fuck you, Dagda. I would prefer to see you suffer."

"I'm already suffering," he muttered, turning away.

It seemed to be forever before he was up in front of the court, his fate meted out. "For the crimes that have led to the near demise of Otherworld, you will spend the rest of your days in the Norse realm of Niflheim. For crimes you have committed on earth, you will be drummed out of our annals forever. It will be as though you never existed."

Dagda didn't flinch, his face impassive as he listened. What did it matter to him where he spent the rest of his days? He was empty, a shell with nothing inside. Nifleheim would be welcome—a place devoid of life and warmth.

As he was being shuffled out in chains Rhiannon appeared, her eyes welling. "Your daughter has appealed to the court, Dagda. If they listen to what she has to say, and take it to heart, you may get a reprieve."

"I do not want a reprieve. Please tell them I plead guilty and will take my punishment." He waved her away.

epilogue

t had been months since Dagda's departure. Kat's one
trip to Otherworld had been done in secrecy, her
hummingbird persona taking her directly to the castle
where the goddesses spent most of their days. She'd
pleaded with Rhiannon and then spent a tear-filled hour
talking with the court officials regarding her father's case.
There had been no sign of whether her pleas had made a
difference. What she'd seen there had shaken her to the
core. The area where the two worlds intersected and
where her dreamscape had been, was gone, leaving behind
a gray wasteland that seemed devoid of oxygen. She hadn't
told Bran what she'd done, or even what she'd seen, sure
that it would have led to an argument, a development she
couldn't cope with.

Kat had opened the safe and taken the government
bonds and cash, as well as her father's instructions written
out in elaborate script. Her mind had twisted with grief
reading his assurances that she could handle the
responsibilities of owning a plane and the rest of his
holdings. A hefty trust had been set up for Siobhan. The
house had mysteriously burned to the ground several days

271

later, the fire Marshall unable to determine the cause.

Kat and Bran moved back to the city where'd they met the first time, settling into the same building. Bran had redone it to resemble the open-floored plan Kat had loved so much the first time, everything exactly as it had been. But this time she shared his bed, her happiness at being together overriding her grief and worry about the future.

Surprisingly, Gwen was still there running Cerridwen's Cosmetic Cauldron. When Kat stopped by and questioned her, she said, "I like it here and I knew you'd be back eventually; this is where you learned about yourself and where your destiny intertwined with Bran's; it's where you fell in love."

It was true. The city was her laughing place, despite everything that had gone on there. "Where's Airmid?"

Gwen's eyes clouded. "She is fighting the Dubh in Otherworld. The destruction they've wrought there is much worse than what they've managed so far on earth. You and Bran are in charge of that fight."

"Why do you say that? I thought with Dagda gone…"

"It was left too long," Gwen answered. "Have you not noticed the blank looks on the faces of those who live here? The Dubh are slowly leaching the light from every living thing. If they are not stopped the people and creatures of earth will be empty as shells and will die off, leaving a colorless world behind."

Kat barely heard her as she glanced out the open door, glad that spring had finally arrived. A breeze wafted in, filled with moisture and the scent of flowers. It would rain today. Mior's first birthday was coming up and her mother had promised to fly out on Dagda's private jet, which now belonged to Kat, the pilot in her employ. Somehow all of this had escaped the FBI's investigations, her father's spells and magics keeping them from seeing what lay right in front of their eyes.

Her father's businesses were still going, the money arriving in the account he'd opened for her. She knew now that Dagda handing over a bunch of cash when she was in Hong Kong was because he wanted to make sure she was able to take care of herself. She didn't know what to make of any of it, wondering if the illegal stuff was still going on or whether the income was legitimate. Unfortunately, Dagda wasn't around to ask. She toyed with the idea of dissolving the corporation, but so far hadn't come to any conclusion. Talking to Bran about it was out of the question. Obviously, he knew about the money. What he didn't know was how much she was getting directly from the ongoing businesses.

Another day, she thought desultorily, her thoughts drifting to the nights spent in Bran's arms. Too soon she would have to face things and perhaps travel to Hong Kong, but for now she needed the respite; after everything she'd been through she wanted to immerse herself in Bran's love for as long as possible.

Her gaze strayed to the men and women walking by on the street, their pale faces blank and expressionless. When she glanced into the far distance the landscape was as gray as the clouds forming in the sky. Her entire body tensed, the sudden realization of what was going on ripping her out of a wonderful dream and throwing her into a nightmare. She'd faced all this weeks before and then put it completely out of her mind, her entire focus on Bran, her mom, and her baby brother.

When Kat turned to Gwen, the goddess nodded, her expression one of resignation. "It is up to you now."

To be continued...

Thank you for reading!

To visit my website: www.nikkibroadwellauthor.com

For news on the release of the next book in the series, or other offerings, please sign up for one of my two newsletters!

https://www.nikkibroadwellauthor.com/
https://www.subscribepage.com/p5w5k1

OTHER BOOKS BY NIKKI:

A Witch in Time Saves Nine
The moon in Her Eyes

The Last Keeper of the Light

Rosemary for Remembrance

Burning Night

Siobhan's Secret—book 1 of
Raven and Hummingbird series

www.ingramcontent.com/pod-product-compliance
Lightning Source LLC
Chambersburg PA
CBHW020418260626
47156CB00007B/2446